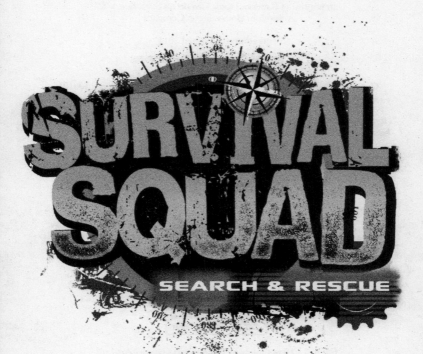

SURVIVAL SQUAD

SEARCH & RESCUE

JONATHAN ROCK

RED FOX

With thanks to Paul May

SURVIVAL SQUAD: SEARCH AND RESCUE
A RED FOX BOOK 978 1 862 30966 1

First published in Great Britain by Red Fox,
an imprint of Random House Children's Publishers UK
A Random House Group Company

This edition published 2012

1 3 5 7 9 10 8 6 4 2

The Random House Group Limited supports the Forest Stewardship Council
(FSC®), the leading international forest certification organization. Our books
carrying the FSC label are printed on FSC® certified paper. FSC is the only forest
certification scheme endorsed by the leading environmental organizations,
including Greenpeace. Our paper procurement policy can be found at
www.randomhouse.co.uk/environment.

Set in 13/19 pt Goudy by Falcon Oast Graphic Art Ltd.

Red Fox Books are published by Random House Children's Publishers UK,
61–63 Uxbridge Road, London W5 5SA

www.randomhousechildrens.co.uk
www.totallyrandombooks.co.uk
www.randomhouse.co.uk

Addresses for companies within The Random House Group Limited can be found
at: www.randomhouse.co.uk/offices.htm

THE RANDOM HOUSE GROUP Limited Reg. No. 954009

A CIP catalogue record for this book is available from the British Library.

Printed and bound in Great Britain by
CPI Group (UK) Ltd, Croydon, CR0 4YY

A MESSAGE FROM
BEAR GRYLLS,
CHIEF SCOUT

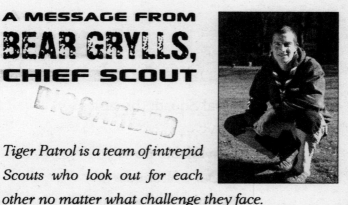

Tiger Patrol is a team of intrepid Scouts who look out for each other no matter what challenge they face.

They've made a promise to do their best and this means picking up skills like navigation, planning, fire lighting and first aid. From moors and woodlands to river rapids, Tiger Patrol is willing to give anything a go – as long as they stay safe.

Scouting is full of great adventures, but you'll only make the most of them if you give everything you've got. You'll need to be alert, committed, trust your friends and never be too proud to ask for help.

Maybe you're already a Scout. If so – be inspired by Tiger Patrol. If you're thinking about joining, then go for it. I did, and I've never looked back.

Are you up for the challenge?

Bear.

Survival Squad: the series

Available now:
Out of Bounds
Search and Rescue

Coming soon:
Night Riders
White Water

CHAPTER 1

Above Abby's head, the helicopter hovered like an enormous orange insect, its powerful blades cutting noisily through the air. A short distance down the icy slope beyond her, the two paramedics finished strapping the casualty onto the stretcher and signalled to the winchman on the helicopter. With one of the paramedics fastened to the cable beside it, the stretcher began to rise slowly into the air, rotating as it went.

Abby lifted a hand and waved as the second paramedic walked towards her.

'Thank you so much, mademoiselle,' he said. 'And you too, monsieur—'

What happened next was lost as the image on Andy's computer screen tilted suddenly, spinning past rows of dark pine trees clinging to near-vertical mountainsides. Andy hit a key and the video began to rewind.

'Andy! What are you doing? We're ready to go.'

Abby Taylor stood in the doorway of her best friend Andy's bedroom. He was bent over his computer, completely absorbed – he seemed to have totally forgotten that tonight was the first Scouts meeting after Christmas.

'I'm editing the footage from the rescue,' he said. 'I won't be long. Look – this is where the paramedic congratulated us and—'

Abby could see herself on the screen, sunglasses pushed back on her forehead, her long hair escaping from a red and white ski hat, caught in the downdraught from the helicopter rotors. 'And you fell over,' she said. 'Obviously I remember. But I'm going to scream in a minute. We have to leave *now* – we're late!'

'The others will never believe we were part of a real helicopter rescue in the Alps,' said Andy, as if he hadn't heard Abby at all. 'I need the video to show them. I'll just edit this bit out and burn it onto a DVD.'

'Andy!' said Abby, exasperated. 'For once your dad is ready, and now *you're* making us late!'

'OK, OK,' said Andy, lifting his hands in surrender. 'I'll just have to show them the footage on the camera. It's lucky it's got such a good display. I'll be there in two minutes.'

Abby shook her head, sighing. 'You won't, you know. You haven't even got your uniform on.'

Andy looked down in surprise at his old jeans and T-shirt, and Abby burst out laughing. It was impossible to stay angry with him for long. 'Looks like we'll just have to be late again. No one will be surprised. Well, go on, then. Get changed. What are you waiting for?'

Three minutes later Andy opened the door, transformed into a rather untidy Scout. His new camcorder was in his hand and he was watching something on the screen. 'It looks fine. This display is incredibly sharp, and it's bright too. Look at this . . .'

'Looks just like any other camcorder to me.'

'You know it's not,' began Andy; then he stopped. 'You're winding me up, aren't you?'

Abby laughed. 'Winding you up is just too easy. Now, can we *please* go?'

She knew how special the camcorder was – of course she did. Andy loved filming and had received the Creative Challenge Award for the film he had made about Tiger Patrol on their last expedition. Abby didn't understand half of what Andy said about his new toy, but she knew he was going to follow in the footsteps of his news cameraman father. Andy was very talented.

In the hallway Andy's mum tried to straighten his collar and tidy his hair, but Abby pushed him out of the door into the freezing January night. 'Sorry, Mrs Mackenzie,' she called over her shoulder. 'We're late!'

Andy's dad was standing by the car, gazing upwards. 'Look at that,' he said. 'What a sky!'

'Mr Mackenzie!' Abby began, but then she looked up and saw the stars. She'd never seen so many, despite the glare from the streetlights. 'Wow! There's the Milky Way!'

'That's our own galaxy,' Andy said. 'Awesome.'

'It's awesome all right,' said Abby, snapping back to reality, 'but not as awesome as Rick and Julie's faces will be when we walk in half an hour late. Can we go now please?'

But when they arrived at Scout HQ, the car park was full of Scouts, and they were standing just like Abby and Andy had ten minutes before, all gazing up at the sky.

Rick, the Scout Leader, and Julie, the Assistant Patrol Leader, waved to the pair and they quickly ran over to find the rest of Tiger Patrol. There was time for only the hastiest of greetings to Connor, the Tigers' athletic, fair-haired Patrol Leader, and to Jay and Priya, the patrol's two newest members. Toby, the dark-haired, wiry Assistant Patrol Leader, was pulling something out of a rucksack.

'Do you take that bag absolutely everywhere?' Priya asked him.

Abby couldn't help noticing that the Tigers' youngest member looked as sharp and cool in her uniform as Andy looked scruffy. 'He always has,' she told Priya. 'Ever since I've known him.'

'*Yes!*' exclaimed Toby. 'I knew they were here somewhere.' He pulled out a pair of binoculars triumphantly.

'OK,' Rick told them. 'This is a great chance to do some work for our Astronomers' Badges. Let's start with the North Star. Can you all see the Plough? The proper name is *Ursa Major*, which means Great Bear – though some people call it the Saucepan. Right now, it's on its side with the handle pointing down, OK?'

'I can't work it out,' complained Priya. 'There are so many stars.'

'I'll show you.' Abby stood beside her and pointed upwards. 'Look – there's the handle, and that's the pan. See?' Priya nodded happily.

'Right,' continued Rick. 'Now find the two stars on the side of the pan that's furthest from the handle. Imagine a line going straight through them and pointing up from the bottom of the saucepan. Follow that line and you'll see a single star, all alone in its own bit of sky.'

'I can see it!' exclaimed Priya.

'That's Polaris,' said Rick, 'the North Star. If you can find the North Star, you'll always know where True North is.'

'Something's wrong with these binoculars,' muttered Toby. 'I was looking at Jupiter and I can't see it any more.' He lowered the binoculars and inspected the lenses.

'It's not your binoculars,' Connor told him. 'It's clouds. They're covering up the stars and planets.'

'Did you see the weather forecast?' Jay asked. 'They said it was going to snow.'

Everyone started talking at once. Abby looked up. Already the stars were fainter – a layer of thin cloud was spreading rapidly across the sky. To the west there were no stars at all any more. She shivered. Recent nights had been frosty, but now the wind was rising and it really was very cold.

'Everyone inside,' called Julie. 'Quick as you

can. There's lots to do.'

Once they were indoors Andy was at last able to show the others his new camcorder. 'It's full HD,' he said, 'and it's got a 180-gigabyte hard drive, but the best thing is the zoom. It's twenty-five times optical, and it's really easy to keep it steady even when you're zoomed right in.' He looked up from the camera. His face, suntanned like Abby's from their skiing holiday, was shining with excitement.

'I didn't understand a word of that,' Connor said, shaking his head. 'It looks great, though.'

'Stop going on about the camera,' interrupted Abby. 'Show them the movie. We just got back from the Alps yesterday,' she told the others. 'We went up on the ski lift and the fog came down, and this stupid man insisted on going off in totally the wrong direction—'

'He wouldn't listen to us,' Andy cut in. 'And because he was a grown-up and he sounded as if he knew what he was doing, my parents and Abby's mum did what he said.'

'It was nearly a disaster,' continued Abby. 'But we had a map and a compass and we got them to stop. Only the man just ignored us, and he kept on going and went over a cliff!'

'Not a very big cliff, luckily,' said Andy. 'Here – you can see.'

The Tigers crowded round to look at the small display screen. Scouts from the other patrols craned their necks to see.

'He didn't fall far,' Abby explained, 'and he landed in a snowdrift. But he broke his leg, and Mum called the Search and Rescue.'

'We gave them a grid reference,' Andy told the assembled Scouts proudly. 'They got to us really fast and took the man to hospital.'

'Didn't you go in the helicopter, then?' asked Kerry, the Kestrels' Patrol Leader.

'No – I wish I had, though,' Andy replied. 'Just think of the footage I could have shot.'

'We skied back,' said Abby. 'I wouldn't have gone in the helicopter anyway. I'd rather ski than do anything else in the world.'

'I guess this is why everyone's calling you Tigers the Survival Squad,' Julie interjected playfully. She and Rick had been listening at the back of the group. 'Everywhere you go, you seem to find trouble!'

'But we don't!' protested Abby.

'I'm teasing,' said Julie. 'Well done for the map–reading, but now we really must get this meeting started.'

The Scouts sat down and Julie began. 'This term we're all going to work towards the Community Challenge Award. There are two parts to it. First, you have to investigate an aspect of your local community and report back about it. It could be learning about a theatre or a dance group – or almost anything where people get together.'

'My karate club,' called out Sajiv, the leader of Panther Patrol.

'My gran goes to bingo,' said Sharon from the Kestrels. 'Would that be OK?'

Everyone laughed, Rick and Julie included.

'Like I said, it could be almost anything,'

continued Julie. 'Best to find out about something you don't know much about already, though, Sajiv. And more fun too. And to get the badge you also have to perform some kind of community service. It's best if that fits with the first part – so, for example, you might find out about local playgrounds and raise some money to buy a new piece of equipment. You might even be able to do some work with the police or the fire service . . . You get the idea. Now I'd like you to go off in your Patrols and talk about what you'd like to do. Think of at least three different ideas. Off you go.'

Connor headed towards the Tigers' den. Photographs of the Sixth Matfield Scout Troop lined the walls, going right back to their foundation in 1927. He knew that they were lucky to have such a big HQ. There was even a room that had been turned into a museum full old camping stoves and billy-cans, uniforms and flags, and thousands of photographs and press cuttings.

'Hey, Connor,' said Jay as they turned to go upstairs. 'Those Sutcliffs on that board – are they anything to do with you?'

The Tigers halted and looked up at the old wooden board on the wall. At the top it said QUEEN'S SCOUTS, and underneath there was a list of names and dates, all picked out in the same gold lettering. 'Well, one of them's my dad,' said Connor.

They all knew Connor's dad. Dr Sutcliff was a parent helper and he never missed a meeting. 'That's him,' Connor told Jay, pointing at the board. 'Chris Sutcliff, 1988. And William Sutcliff's my grandpa. He became a Queen's Scout in 1964.'

Jay pointed to the empty space waiting for new Queen's Scouts. 'I suppose you want to have your name up there too?'

Connor looked at him suspiciously. When Jay first started Scouts he had hated every minute of it – and he'd hated Connor most of all. Just for a second Connor wondered if Jay was laughing at him. But then he realized that his new friend was serious. 'Yeah, it would be quite cool,' he admitted, 'but it's not that easy.'

'You can say that again,' put in Toby. 'Even if you have a Gold Duke of Edinburgh Award, that's only part of it. You—'

'Hey, Tigers!' Connor's dad was coming down the corridor. 'What are you doing? You should have started by now.'

'It's OK, Dad,' Connor explained. 'Jay wanted to know about Queen's Scouts.'

'Oh, well,' said his dad. 'I'm glad you're interested, Jay. I'm sure Toby and Connor can tell you all you need to know. I think Toby knows *The Scout Handbook* by heart.'

'Only some of it.' It was Toby's turn to look embarrassed, and the others laughed. 'But you've actually done it, Chris. Can't you tell us about it?'

'I'd love to,' said Connor's dad, 'but not right now. Me and Connor's grandpa are hoping we'll soon have another Sutcliff up there, though. Right, Connor?'

'Maybe.' Connor gave his dad a meaningful look, hoping he would understand, but Dr Sutcliff didn't seem to notice. Connor sighed inwardly; he knew his friends all liked his dad – he could be a lot of fun – but he wished he would learn when to keep quiet.

He quickly led the way to the den. It was little more than a store cupboard really. There was an assortment of camping equipment squashed in by the small square window, but there was still just room for the six Tigers to sit on stools. Pinned to the notice board were photos of the Tigers at last year's camp, and of their adventure last term when they went orienteering on the moors. Andy was a terrific photographer. A huge black-and-white print showed the members of Tiger Patrol walking up a hillside and melting into grey mist as they tried to find their way back to the check-point. For a moment Connor felt as if he was there again.

'It was scary,' said Priya, looking at the photo-graph of Connor and Toby helping Abby to climb down a cliff beside a waterfall. 'But I'd do it again like a shot. It's the most exciting thing I've ever done.'

'You were a natural on the rocks,' Connor said with a smile. 'Maybe we'll do some more climbing this summer. But right now we'd better get started.'

He took a notepad from a cupboard on the wall. A picture on the cupboard door (drawn by Andy) showed a savage tiger and a death's head. Under the picture was written:

TIGER PATROL
DANGER – KEEP OUT!

'Right, has anyone got any ideas for this Community Challenge badge?'

No one replied. They were all staring out of the window. Big flakes of snow were floating down. 'Do you think it's going to settle?' asked Abby.

Andy stood up and pushed some tent poles out

of the way so he could see better. 'Looks like it,' he reported. 'The car park's turning white already.'

'We still have to do this,' insisted Connor, although he was just as excited as the rest of them. 'We have to think of something to find out about.'

'There's the skate park,' Jay suggested. 'The one at the end of my road. It's a real mess.'

'We'd have to talk to skateboarders,' said Abby. 'It might be fun.'

'I'll write it down,' said Connor. 'Rick said we should have three ideas. Anyone else?'

Andy stopped fiddling with his camcorder for a moment and looked up. 'How about the police? I saw a thing on the TV about some Scouts helping them catch speeding drivers. The drivers could either pay a fine or have a safety talk from a Scout. That might be cool.'

The others agreed, and Connor noted the idea down.

'Couldn't we find out about Search and

Rescue?' suggested Priya. 'Like the people Abby and Andy saw in the Alps?'

'Do they have Search and Rescue here?' asked Abby doubtfully. 'It's not as if there are mountains.'

'They must do,' Andy said. 'There are the moors, after all. They would have called them out if we hadn't found our way home.'

The Tigers began to talk excitedly. 'Maybe they'll take us up in a helicopter,' Andy said. 'I really wanted to go with them, you know. Just think of the aerial shots I would have got.'

'Excellent,' said Connor. 'That's three great ideas. Brilliant, Priya!'

'It was, wasn't it?' she replied with a grin.

The door opened and Dr Sutcliff's head appeared. 'How's it going?' he asked. 'Any brilliant ideas?'

'They're all brilliant, of course,' replied Abby. 'But Priya's is the best. We want to try and find out about the people who do Search and Rescue.'

'Very good,' said Connor's dad approvingly.

'You know what? I might just be able to help you with that.'

'What did he mean?' Abby said, when Dr Sutcliff had gone.

'No idea,' replied Connor. 'You know my dad. He loves surprises.'

'Hey, listen,' interrupted Andy. 'What's that noise?'

They were all silent for a moment. Outside, the wind was howling around the eaves of the old building and rattling the windows. Large snowflakes pattered against the glass.

'It's a blizzard,' said Toby.

Andy climbed onto a stool and wiped the condensation off the window. 'I can't see a thing,' he said. 'It's a total whiteout.'

The door opened and Rick put his head into the den. 'Everyone in the hall. We're calling your parents. They're going to come and get you now. If they don't, we'll probably be stuck here all night.'

CHAPTER 2

'Now, listen,' said Rick when the Scouts were all gathered in the hall. 'We're hoping for a lull in the storm. Chris and Julie are on the phone to your parents right now, and as soon as the snow lets up they'll be here to collect you.'

'The weather forecast didn't predict a blizzard like this,' said Jay. 'It's really wild out there.'

'I know,' said Rick as a ferocious gust of wind battered Scout HQ with a noise like thunder. 'If this keeps up we'll be trying for Snowsports Badges instead of the Community Challenge.'

'Wouldn't that be great!?' Abby turned to the other Tigers as Rick went off to help with the phoning. 'Me and Andy could teach you all to ski. We could be the Tiger Ski Patrol.'

'Not me,' said Toby. 'Before Christmas my

mum took me ice-skating on the rink outside the town hall. I fell over about a million times.'

'I love skating,' said Priya. 'My brother is rubbish, though. It was great watching him fall over. It was his own fault. He wouldn't let me give him lessons.'

Abby could see that the others just didn't get it. 'Skiing isn't like skating,' she told them. 'It's like . . . flying.' She was remembering the descent back to the resort on the afternoon of the rescue. It seemed incredible that it had taken place only a few short days ago. She could almost feel the cold clean air on her face; almost see the dazzle of the brilliant sunshine; the amazing sensation as the edge of her ski bit into new snow and she flew down the mountainside.

'It is awesome, really it is,' agreed Andy. 'Me and Abby have been lucky. We've been going with our families ever since we were little.'

'We're going again later this year,' Abby said. 'To Norway. We've never been there before.' It had felt a bit odd hearing Andy talking about when they were little, going with their parents. It was just her and her mum now, and she should be used to that because it was years and years since they'd all gone together. Her dad had given her her first skiing lessons, and sometimes she really missed him. She told herself she was being silly. It wasn't as if she didn't see him lots . . .

'Hey, listen,' said Connor. 'It's gone quiet.'

Sure enough, the wind had dropped. Toby went to the door and opened it. The Scouts went out into a changed world. Everything was white. The snow had stopped falling and the bushes around the edge of the car park were rounded white lumps. The entrance was blocked by drifts of snow. A car passed down the street, moving very slowly.

Toby bent down and dug his hands into the drift. 'It's perfect,' he said, pressing the snow into a ball and turning to the others. 'It couldn't be better for a snowball fight!'

The snowballs flew thick and fast.

*

When Connor awoke the next morning, he sensed an unusual brightness in the room. He jumped up, pulled the curtains back and looked out on a silent white garden. The snowfall had been very heavy, obliterating the outlines of paths and driveways. The house was quiet. He dressed quickly and raced downstairs to find his grandpa already up and making a pot of tea in the kitchen. His grandparents lived in Manchester, where his grandpa taught at the university; his grandma was a doctor, like Connor's dad. They had been staying for the New Year.

'We're snowed in,' said his grandpa, clearly pleased. 'Me and your grandma won't be going home today after all.'

As Connor opened the front door, his grandpa came up behind him. He handed Connor his wellies. 'Here. I think you're going to need these!'

Connor pulled on the boots and took a couple of steps. His feet sank in deeply – the snow nearly came over the top of the boots. With each step he had to lift his foot high and plant it down again. It was impossible to stop the powdery snow finding its way into his wellies, but he kept going until he was standing outside the gate. He turned round and saw that his grandpa was still watching from the doorway.

'There are no cars, Grandpa,' he said. Out in the road there were no tyre tracks. The only marks were the tiny trails of birds' footprints. There was more snow than Connor had ever seen.

'Oi, Connor!' He looked up and saw his older sister, Ellie, leaning out of her bedroom window. 'I hate you,' she yelled. 'I wanted to be first.'

Connor pulled a face at her. He made his way slowly back to the front door, trying to walk in his own deep footsteps. Ellie was fifteen, and she liked to make out she was all grown up these days, but sometimes she still acted like a kid. He couldn't wait to get her with a snowball. As he went inside, he caught a delicious whiff of bacon – everyone was up now, and his grandma was already making breakfast.

'You're going to need plenty to eat,' she said to Connor. 'I bet you'll be outside all day.'

'Quiet a minute.' Connor's dad was listening to the radio. 'I want to hear the news.'

'*Exceptionally heavy overnight snowfall has brought most of England and Wales to a standstill this morning,*' said the newsreader. '*Central areas of England are the worst affected, and in many places all main roads are completely impassable. Airports are closed and rail services have been suspended. Police are urging motorists not to venture out unless their journey is absolutely necessary.*'

'Well, that's it, then,' Dr Sutcliff said. 'No chance of you going home today, Dad.'

'I never thought there was. Your sledge is all ready for you, Connor. I've been out in the garage waxing the runners. I thought maybe I'd come out with you.'

Connor stood up, but his dad put a hand on his arm. 'Hold on, Connor – I've got some news about your Search and Rescue project. A few months back, a guy called Rob came into the

surgery asking for volunteers for a local Search
and Rescue team. So I called him last night and
he said they were meeting today. I told him about
your project, and he was very keen to meet you.
He said you could all go along to the meeting this
morning, but I'd better check that it's still on
with all this snow.'

'Cool. Thanks, Dad. But I ought to ask the
others if it's what they want to do.'

'You can ask now.' Dr Sutcliff was looking out
of the window. 'One of them has just arrived!'

Connor ran to the front door and the rest of
the family followed him. Abby was standing
outside, her face flushed and her eyes shining. 'I
skied from my house,' she said. 'It was downhill
all the way and it's the most perfect powder
snow.'

'Where's Andy?' asked Connor as she bent to
take off her skis.

'Oh, he's behind me somewhere.' Abby waved
airily back up the road. 'He couldn't ski because
he's pulling the sledge.'

Just then Andy plodded into sight. 'Next time I'm doing the skiing,' he said. 'That was hard work.'

'We couldn't wait.' Abby planted her skis upright in the snow. 'It's just so perfect. We didn't see a car moving anywhere. Why aren't you ready? We're wasting time.'

'You'll have to wait a few minutes,' Connor said. 'We haven't had breakfast yet. Come in. I expect there's enough for you.'

'We've had breakfast already,' Abby said. 'But I expect we could eat another one.'

'Too right!' agreed Andy.

Five minutes later they were all sitting round the big kitchen table when Dr Sutcliff came into the room with the phone in his hand. 'We're on,' he announced. 'The Search and Rescue team are meeting at the church hall on Albert Street. If you can get there by nine o'clock, they'll tell you all about the work they do before the meeting starts.'

'What's he talking about?' asked Abby.

Connor explained. 'But that's perfect!' she said, spearing a sausage on her fork. 'It's just what we wanted.'

'We haven't asked Toby, Jay and Priya yet,' said Connor.

'Well, ask them, then.' Abby pushed back her chair and got to her feet. 'I'll do it if you like. Can I use your phone please, Mrs Sutcliff? They're going to love this.'

Connor exchanged a look with Andy, and they both laughed. 'Just let her get on with it,' Andy said. 'You know you can't stop her. This bacon is delicious, Mrs Sutcliff.'

A few minutes later Abby returned. 'They all agreed,' she announced. 'And Jay's asked us all to go back to his house for lunch. Come on, you two. We have to get ready. It's going to be hard work. Skis are useless on the flat, especially on this powder snow.'

'Of course, that's not a problem with Norwegian cross-country skis,' said Connor's grandpa. 'They'd be perfect in these conditions.

Did I ever tell you about the time I crossed the Hardangervidda in the steps of Amundsen? It was—'

'Grandpa! You can tell us later,' said Connor, shaking his head good-naturedly. 'If we're going to this meeting, we don't want to be late.'

'Fair enough.' Connor's grandpa's eyes glinted as he picked up the newspaper. 'If you don't want to see the skis I brought with me, it's no skin off my nose.'

'You brought skis? But why . . . ?'

Connor's grandpa stood up and stretched, and then his weather-beaten face broke into a smile. 'When I saw the long-range forecast before Christmas, I knew there was a chance something like this would happen,' he told them. 'There are four pairs of cross-country skis for you lot to use. They're old, but they'll do the job.'

'But we'll need special boots, won't we?' asked Abby.

Connor saw his grandpa's eyes twinkling again. 'I wasn't a Queen's Scout for nothing,' he said. 'I know how to plan ahead. I had Chris do a little research on shoe sizes. I think you'll be all right.'

'You're brilliant,' Grandpa,' Connor said. 'But you went to a lot of trouble when you couldn't even be sure it would snow.'

'I love cross-country skiing,' his grandpa replied. 'I wasn't going to miss a chance to show you lot how to do it. I might even try to convert you, Abby!'

'No chance,' Abby replied. 'But I wouldn't mind having a go.'

'Me and your dad'll come to this meeting with you and show you how to use the skis afterwards,' Connor's grandpa said. 'It's hard work, but a lot of fun. They're in the garage with the sledge. Let's go and fetch them.'

The Tigers followed Connor's grandpa outside and helped him to lift the sledge out of the garage. 'It's huge!' exclaimed Abby.

'And old,' said Andy.

'That's right.' Connor's grandpa stroked the

smooth wood affectionately. 'My dad made it for me when I was a boy. We could get four people on it. But you'll have to watch out on the hill – it's fast! Look – these are the skis.' He laid a canvas bag down on top of the sledge and pulled out two long, narrow wooden skis.

'They look ancient,' said Abby. 'Are you sure they still work?'

'Of course. I've waxed them with the right wax. You have to use different wax for different temperatures, you know.'

'We do know,' laughed Abby as Connor's grandpa put the skis away and strapped the bag to the sledge.

'Now, I've got my own skis here,' he told them, 'and there's my reserve pair for Chris. We'll show you what these things can do. Connor and Andy, you get on the big sledge with all the skis. Chris will pull you. Abby, get on that one. I'll be your dog team!'

'Cool,' said Abby. 'Can I yell at you?'

'Sure thing.' Connor's grandpa clipped his

boots into a gleaming pair of skis. 'I believe "*mush*" is the word you want!'

'Mush!' cried Abby. 'Mush! Mush! Let's go, dogs!'

Connor's dad and grandpa laughed as they took up the strain on the ropes, and the two sledges began to move forward, slowly at first, and then with increasing speed. The Tigers moved off through the snow-covered streets.

CHAPTER 3

'You're in great shape, aren't you, Grandpa?' said Connor twenty minutes later, when they arrived at the church hall, having collected the other Tigers on the way.

'Of course I am!' His grandpa smiled. 'I'm not so sure about your dad, though! I think he was puffing a bit at the end there!' He gave Dr Sutcliff a friendly shove.

'Hey!' protested Connor's dad. 'You're the one who was having trouble keeping up.'

Connor rolled his eyes comically and turned to the others. Toby and Priya were both hauling Toby's sledge, but they'd found it hard going pulling it through the snow, sinking nearly to their knees each time they took a step forward.

'That was tough,' grunted Toby as he took his rucksack off his sledge.

'We need skis like theirs,' said Priya, looking enviously at Connor's dad and grandpa. 'It was easy for them.'

'Not that easy,' Connor told her quietly. 'My dad's really out of breath, although he's trying not to let on.'

'But you *are* going to have skis,' Abby burst out, unable to contain herself any longer. 'Connor's grandpa brought them with him, and boots too. We're going try them when we go to the park after this.'

Priya, Toby and Jay all wanted to know more, but the door of the hut opened and a tall man with untidy red hair and a beard greeted them with a smile. 'You must be Tiger Patrol,' he said. 'I'm Rob. Come on in – the others are already here. Some of us walked, and luckily I've got a four-by-four.'

Inside the hut they found two women and two men seated in a semicircle around an open laptop on a table. They all stood up, smiling, as the Scouts came in.

'I'll introduce you,' Rob said. 'Evie and Soraya, Pete and Gerry, meet Tiger Patrol.'

Pete was tall and rangy, with a lopsided grin. His friend Gerry was stocky and muscular, with a shaven head – Connor thought he looked about the same age as his grandpa. The two women were much younger – both of them were tanned and fit-looking. All the volunteers were wearing orange fleeces with the words ALSAR, MATFIELD on the front.

'OK, everyone,' said Rob when the Scouts had all sat down. 'We're the local ALSAR group. That stands for Association of Lowland Search and Rescue. We're all volunteers, and it's our job to help the emergency services to find missing persons and sometimes to carry out rescues. I'm sure you've all seen people like us on the TV when there's been a big search for someone who's gone missing, and you probably haven't even realized who we are.'

'But . . . is this all of you?' asked Abby, unable to hide her surprise and disappointment.

Rob grimaced. 'We feel the same way you do,' he said. 'We desperately need to find more volunteers, and we're wondering if you might be able to help us.'

'Of course we will!' Abby turned expectantly to the other Tigers. 'We'll all volunteer, won't we? Me and Andy have already helped with a mountain rescue in the Alps.'

Rob laughed and shook his head. 'Sorry, guys. You have to be eighteen to volunteer. But what we're hoping is – maybe you can get us some publicity. Chris tells me you're doing some kind of community project.'

'It's perfect!' exclaimed Andy. 'We could make a film about you.'

'Right,' agreed Toby with enthusiasm. 'We could show it to the parents of everyone who comes to Scouts. Some of them are bound to want to volunteer.'

'But what do you actually do?' asked Connor.

'Good question,' replied Evie. 'We're trained to look for people who go missing. We were called out twice last month to look for old people who'd got themselves lost. And we found them too.'

'But . . . it's not just old people you look for, is it?' asked Jay.

'No,' replied Soraya. 'People go missing for all kinds of reasons. Earlier this year there was a massive search when a little boy disappeared. ALSAR teams from all over the country helped to find him.'

'Right now we're planning a training exercise in the snow for next weekend,' said Pete. 'It's not often we get a chance to practise navigation skills in really deep snow. Hey, maybe you'd like to come along? We could even set up some special challenges for you – see how you get on.'

Connor looked at his dad.

'Your decision, Tigers,' Dr Sutcliff said.

'Where would it take place?' asked Connor.

'We've arranged to use the country park,' Rob

replied. 'It should be fine, as long as the weather holds.'

'Cool,' said Abby. 'We did orienteering there.'

'You'll find it looks a bit different in the snow,' warned Rob. 'You'll be surprised.'

'I can make it then,' said Toby. The other Tigers all nodded agreement.

'Well, thanks,' said Connor. 'We'd love to do it. But I've been thinking – couldn't the rest of our Troop come too? I bet they'd love it.'

'Excellent,' said Rob. 'The more the merrier.'

'I'll call Rick and see what he thinks,' said Connor's dad. 'Great idea, Connor.'

'I'll film everything.' Andy was already reaching for his camcorder as Dr Sutcliff went off to make the call. 'And I'll need to interview you, so you can explain all the things you do. I could start now, if you like.'

The Search and Rescue team looked at each other for a moment, then all broke into big smiles. 'I have a feeling you're just what we need,' said Rob. 'We'd love to do the interviews, wouldn't we, guys?' The team all agreed with enthusiasm. 'But before we do that,' he continued, 'we planned a little first-aid test for you. Are you up for it?'

'Of course we are!' said Abby. 'I don't mind going first. What do we have to do?'

Rob was whispering in Soraya's ear. She nodded and went to the far end of the hall, then disappeared through a door into a back room. 'Soraya's going to be the first victim,' Rob told them. 'You have all done some first-aid training, right?' The Tigers nodded. 'OK, then. Off you go, Abby. The rest of us will watch from a safe distance.'

They all followed Abby as she made her way across the hall and through the door.

'I think that was a clue,' Toby muttered to Connor. 'The bit about watching from a safe distance, I mean. I saw Rob wink at Pete.'

'I don't think Abby noticed,' replied Connor. 'Here goes.'

The back room turned out to be a kitchen. A

cupboard on the wall held stacks of cups and plates, and a cooker and work-surface lined the far wall. Soraya was lying on the floor near the cooker, her black hair hiding her face.

Abby rushed across the room and knelt beside her. 'Soraya,' she said. 'Can you hear me?'

She reached out a hand and took hold of Soraya's shoulder, shaking her gently. 'Can you hear me?' she repeated.

'I'm going to stop you there, Abby,' Rob said, crossing the floor to join her. 'Unfortunately, you're dead! Or at least very seriously injured. Can anyone tell Abby why?'

'There's a wire,' Toby pointed out. 'She's lying on top of it. You forgot to check for danger.'

Abby hit the palm of her hand against her forehead. 'I don't believe it,' she said as Soraya climbed to her feet, revealing a small electric heater. 'I *knew* I should have checked for danger, but I just wanted to get on with it.'

'Exactly,' said Rob, smiling. 'DRABC. Danger, Response, Airway, Breathing and Circulation. It's important to act quickly, but don't miss out any of the steps. The first one's just as important as the others. If there's been an accident, then something's caused it, and you have to make sure the same thing can't happen to you. OK, who's next? We've thought up some tricky ones for you.'

When they left the church hall an hour later, the Tigers were all buzzing with excitement. They had identified a broken arm, a possible fractured pelvis and a dangerous spinal injury, and Abby had cheered up considerably when Evie had praised her for remembering why it was important to keep giving cardiac compressions to a patient who wasn't breathing.

'You don't stop until the ambulance arrives,' she'd said. 'It keeps up the oxygen supply to the brain.'

'That bit was good,' Andy said as they headed for the park. 'But of course you should already have been dead.'

Abby launched a friendly kick at him, but he jumped nimbly out of her way. 'The interviews were great too,' he said, laughing. 'We've found out loads already. I reckon we're a cert for the Community Challenge Award.'

Dr Sutcliff left them when they reached the park. 'Your grandpa's the cross-country skiing expert,' he told Connor. 'He won't need my help, and there's a patient I'd like to call in on. See you later.'

'Hey, Dad,' Connor called after him as he skied off. 'Thanks for organizing the Search and Rescue thing.'

'No worries.' Connor's dad paused. 'It's a terrific thing to do. And I thought you did really well with the first aid. But you'd better go, Connor. I think your grandpa wants to get started on the skiing lessons! Good luck!'

Abby couldn't help feeling a little disappointed when she saw that the park was already crowded with people. It was the best hill in Matfield for sledging, and it seemed as if half the children in the town were already there. Abby saw several people she knew from school. They were careering down the hill on every sort of sledge and tray, and even on plastic rubbish sacks. She spotted Ellie, Connor's sister, wearing a bright pink puffa jacket and a hat with tiger stripes and a tail hanging down behind. Abby thought she looked cool, but Connor rolled his eyes when he saw what she was wearing.

'And I bet she'll want to use our sledge,' he said.

Priya was looking up at the hill. 'I don't think so,' she told him. 'There's my brother.'

Mihir careered down the slope on a small tea-tray, crashing into a snowdrift at Ellie's feet. He stood up, laughing, and the two of them ran off back up the hill together.

'Phew!' said Connor. 'That's lucky,'

'Maybe it's love!' said Priya, grinning cheekily at him. 'I knew Mihir liked your sister.'

'Are you all ready?' asked Connor's grandpa. 'I

want to give you a skiing lesson, then I'm away home for my lunch.'

He took them to a flat area where the snow had hardly been touched. The boots that he took from a rucksack fitted them perfectly, and as Abby and Andy looked on, he showed Connor, Jay, Priya and Toby how to fasten them into the long Norwegian skis. 'This won't be perfect,' he warned them, 'but the snow here isn't too deep and you should be able to have some fun. The most important thing to remember is to keep your weight forward. Then try taking small walking steps, and each time you take a step let yourself glide a little.'

'But your heels come up off the skis,' said Abby, who was watching his feet, fascinated, but impatient to be skiing herself. 'On mine my whole foot is fastened down.'

'That's right.' Connor's grandpa did a little dance on his skis. 'It's very different from downhill skiing. Wait a moment. I'll just put my wellies on and you can have a go on these,

Abby. My feet are only a little bigger than yours.'

Seconds later Abby found herself trying to walk and glide forward on cross-country skis, while Andy stood back and filmed everything. Time after time the Scouts overbalanced backwards in the snow and Connor's grandpa patiently showed them how to push themselves upright again.

'It's all good practice,' he said, laughing. 'That's lesson number two – how to get back on your feet! I'll have those skis back now please, Abby – I'm off for my lunch. Enjoy yourselves.'

'We'll go on a journey to get some practice,' Connor said. 'Across the park and back.'

'Not me,' said Abby, taking her own skis off the sledge. 'I'm going to do some proper skiing. Coming, Andy?'

'Don't let my grandpa hear you saying that,' said Connor. 'See you back here.'

Abby found that she needed all her skill to ski downhill through the crowds of sledgers. It was nothing like the Alps, but it was still a lot more fun than cross-country skiing.

'Can you believe it?' she said to Andy when they paused for a moment at the top of the hill. Her eyes were shining. 'We're actually skiing in Matfield.'

'I'll race you to the bottom,' said Andy. 'And this time I'm going to beat you. Hey! Wait! That's not fair.'

Abby laughed as she zigzagged down the hill. Andy reached the bottom just seconds behind her. 'I would have beaten you if you hadn't cheated,' he began.

But Abby was pointing at the returning Tigers. 'They look exhausted,' she said.

'It's a lot harder than it looks,' Priya told Abby when she arrived, stretching and grimacing.

'We ought to stop now anyway,' said Jay. 'My mum said we should be home for lunch by two at the latest. She makes the best shepherd's pie in the world, and there's chocolate fudge pudding too!'

'We can go out the other way,' Connor said, pointing to the far corner of the park. 'It's shorter.'

Abby moved off ahead. The others had tried to haul their sledges while wearing skis and discovered that it was far harder than Connor's dad and grandpa had made it look. They were now plodding along with the skis strapped to the sledges, but Abby was gliding smoothly down the gentle slope towards the exit. Skiing on the crowded hill had been a challenge, but what they really needed was a place with no other people—

Loud shouts interrupted her thoughts. She came to a halt in a little flurry of snow. Ahead of her she saw a wide flat area where the snow was largely undisturbed. A small group of teenagers were gathered there, watching as one boy ran towards the flat part and slid over it, ploughing a pathway through the snow.

'That's a pond,' said Jay, coming up beside her. 'They'll fall in. And it'll serve them right.'

Abby glanced at him, and then back at the

pond. The boy who had been sliding got to his feet and turned back to look at his friends. Abby knew him at once. His name was Lee – and there, standing with the others, were two more people she recognized – Vicky and Sean. A couple of months earlier, Tiger Patrol had come to their rescue: Sean had fallen off his bike up on the moors, and broken his arm. Now it looked as if they might need rescuing again at any moment.

Connor caught up with Abby and Jay. 'What's happening?' he asked them.

Abby pointed to the pond. 'They're bound to go through. The cold weather only started a few days ago. It hasn't had time to freeze properly.'

'There was a heron fishing on the far side yesterday afternoon,' said Andy. 'I've got video to prove it. Most of it was frozen, but there was still some open water.'

'Let's just leave them to it,' muttered Jay. 'They won't listen to us anyway.'

'We have to say something,' said Toby, bringing his sledge to a halt beside the others.

'I know they're a pain in the neck, Jay, but I was talking to Evie at the meeting earlier. She said that even if the water's not very deep you can still get trapped under the ice.'

'It's unbelievably stupid,' said Abby. She knew these kids didn't really deserve their help. They had bullied Jay when he'd first started secondary school, and she didn't want to talk to them. But she also knew that if they fell in, then other people might have to risk their lives going to rescue them. They had to be stopped. She took a deep breath and walked towards them, calling out as she went. Then she realized that Connor was right beside her.

'Get off there!' he yelled. 'It's not safe. The ice is too thin.'

The group all turned towards the Scouts. Lee pushed Sean out of the way and stepped forward. 'Are you talking to me?' he said to Connor and Abby.

'Who else would we be talking to?' Abby replied. She glanced at Connor; he was standing next to her, tall and calm. Her confidence grew. 'My friend was here yesterday,' she told the boys, indicating Andy, who was coming towards them. 'He saw the ice. It'll never hold you.'

'Go on, Sean,' said Lee, all the time staring at Connor's face. 'Have a go.'

Sean took a few paces backwards and then raced onto the frozen pond and slid along the track that Lee had made. At the end he ploughed a couple of metres further out onto the ice. His friends cheered as he got to his feet, laughing.

'See?' sneered Lee. 'You don't know what you're talking about, do you? So why don't you all shove off and do whatever it is sad little Scouts do.'

Abby opened her mouth to speak, but Connor put a hand on her arm. 'Abby was trying to help you,' he said, his voice coldly furious.

'Yeah? Well, she can just go and help someone else, OK?'

Abby turned to walk away, but suddenly she saw a little girl running around, in and out of the gang of teenagers. 'You can't let her go on the ice,' she said to Lee. 'What if she falls in?'

'What are you, deaf or something?' he replied. 'That's my little sister and she won't fall in, not while I'm here. If me and Sean can go on the ice, then she can too. You want to argue about it?'

Lee stopped forward threateningly. Connor didn't move. He held the boy's gaze until he looked away and spat on the snow. Abby held her breath as the little girl skidded onto the ice, fell over, and then picked herself up, squealing with delight.

'Forget it, Abby,' Connor said disgustedly as Lee turned his back on them and went back to join his mates. 'There's no way we're ever going to stop them.'

CHAPTER 4

Connor could still hear the shouts of Lee and his friends echoing from the park as they made their way across the road. The snow was now lumpy and rutted from the tracks made by feet and sledges and occasional cars.

Abby came up beside him. 'How could they be so stupid?' she said. 'What if the ice gives way? We should call the police. Dial nine-nine-nine.'

'Let's hope it doesn't give way,' replied Connor. 'We can't call nine-nine-nine. It's not actually an emergency. Not yet, anyway.'

'Well, we should tell someone. It makes me really angry. If they fall in, someone's going to have to try and rescue them.'

'You're right. I'll call my dad when we get to Jay's house. He'll know what to do.'

'Look,' interrupted Priya, indicating with her head. 'There are some police officers. We can tell them.'

'Actually,' Toby said, 'they're PCSOs.'

Priya looked confused.

'Police Community Support Officers,' he explained. 'I'm not sure if they can arrest anyone.'

'They wouldn't need to arrest them,' said Abby. 'They just have to make them stop.'

'Whatever you call them, Lee won't like it,' said Jay, frowning. 'Are you sure that ice was sketchy, Andy? It seemed OK when they were on it.'

'You saw what was happening,' Andy told him. 'Every time that slide they were making gets a bit longer, they're getting nearer to the part that wasn't frozen yesterday. Hey, wait a minute – I can show you.'

He took out his camcorder and turned it on. 'Look at this' – he pointed at the screen – 'you can see the patch of open water perfectly. That was only yesterday afternoon. There's no way it's properly frozen.'

'I agree,' said Priya, her dark eyes full of concern.

'I guess you're right,' conceded Jay. 'I don't much care what happens to Lee, but there were little kids there.'

'I don't know what you're all waiting for,' said Abby impatiently. 'They shouldn't be playing on a frozen pond anyway. I'm going to tell them.'

She crossed the road and approached the PCSOs. 'Please,' she said, the words tumbling out rapidly. 'There are some kids on the pond in the park. They're making a slide and we tried to warn them but they wouldn't stop. They've got a little girl with them too. I'm worried something terrible might happen.'

'Hey, now, hold on a minute.' The officer who spoke was tall and thin with a nose like a beak. His voice was kind and calm. 'Just slow down and tell us exactly what you saw. My name's Ray, by the way, and this young lady's Barbara.'

The second officer was the exact opposite of the man – small and round with blond curls exploding from under her hat.

'We weren't sure what to do,' explained Connor, joining Abby. 'There hasn't actually been an accident yet, but Abby's right. It was dangerous, what they were doing.'

'You did exactly the right thing,' said Ray. 'We were told this morning to keep a special eye on the ponds and rivers. Come on, Babs, we'd best get a move on. Thanks, kids.'

The two officers headed off down the road, half jogging, half stumbling as they followed the trail left by the Scouts.

'OK,' Connor said. 'Now we really have done everything we possibly can. I'm ready to try your mum's shepherd's pie, Jay.'

They turned the corner into Jay's road, and were nearly at his house when they saw an elderly lady standing in her doorway, shaking her head. 'I've never seen so much snow,' she said. 'Not since 1963. I can't even get to the letter box.'

'Have you got a spade, Mrs Holmes?' asked Jay. 'We could clear the path for you – couldn't we, you lot?'

'Sure,' replied Connor with a grin. He was impressed that Jay was so keen. He really had changed a lot in the last few months. 'Do you have any salt Mrs Holmes? It'll make sure the driveway doesn't ice over.'

'See,' said Jay. 'The Scouts think of everything, Mrs H. You can trust us.'

Connor looked over at Jay, who winked at him and smiled teasingly.

'You're all very kind to do this,' said Mrs Holmes. 'I'll just fetch a shovel.' She disappeared into her house.

'But I'm starving,' groaned Andy. 'I was looking forward to that shepherd's pie. My mum and dad never cook anything like that.'

'You wait till you taste the chocolate fudge pudding,' said Jay.

'This won't take long,' said Connor. 'We can take it in turns.' He waded up Mrs Holmes's path, took the shovel from her when she reappeared in the doorway, and began to dig.

'Here, let me,' said Priya eagerly, after he'd cleared a short stretch. She began flinging the snow to one side, and the others all laughed at her enthusiasm.

Connor was right. It only took a few minutes to clear the path. When they'd finished, Mrs Holmes came out and pressed a packet of sweets into Connor's hand. 'I insist,' she said when he tried to refuse.

'Well, thanks,' he said, showing the packet to the others as a shout came from down the road.

'Hey, Jay. I hope you're going to do our path too.'

Connor turned and saw Jay's mum waving at them from the small front garden of his house. She was wearing a red apron with a picture of Robbie Williams on it, and her hair, which had been long and blond last time he'd seen it, was now short and dark. But her infectious smile was still the same.

'We'll do it, Mum,' Jay called back. 'But we're all starving. Can we have our lunch first, please?'

'Come on, then,' Mrs Watson said, laughing. 'Let's get you all fed. Have you had a good morning?'

'More chocolate fudge pudding, Connor?' asked Jay's mum. 'How about a little cream with it?'

'No thanks, Mrs Watson,' answered Connor, leaning back and patting his stomach. 'The shepherd's pie was fantastic and I've already had two helpings of pudding. I think I'm going to burst. It was really delicious, but I had a huge breakfast.'

'Stop grumbling,' laughed Andy. 'We had *two* breakfasts. I'm going to have a bit more.'

The friends were sitting around Jay's kitchen table looking at the remains of the delicious sticky pudding.

'You can't,' Abby said to Andy. 'It's nearly three o'clock already and it gets dark really early, and we still have to clear Jay's path.'

'I'm not sure I can move,' said Andy.

'Well, you've got to,' said Jay. 'You have to pay for your lunch. Right, Mum?'

Mrs Watson laughed. 'The lunch is free,' she said. 'But I would love it if you could do the path.'

They made their way outside and set to work. They'd nearly finished when they heard a voice calling them. Connor looked up and saw a woman's face at the upstairs window of a house opposite. 'Will you do mine?' she shouted. 'I'll pay you.'

Connor looked at the others. 'How about it?' he said. 'I bet it'll count towards our Community Challenge.'

'Especially if I get it all on video,' said Andy.

'Don't think you're going to get out of the hard work that way,' Abby told him.

'I won't be,' Andy replied. 'Think of all the hours I have to spend editing it afterwards. I bet that's ten times as hard as shovelling a bit of snow.'

'You don't have to film all the time, though,'

Connor said. 'In fact, you can have first go with the shovel! We'll have it done in five minutes,' he called up to the lady in the window. 'You don't have to pay us a thing. Come on, Andy.'

Before the Tigers had finished, two more of Jay's neighbours had emerged from their houses and were watching them work. Abby heaved the last shovelful onto the pile and stood up, stretching her back. 'Oh, no!' she said when she saw the onlookers. 'They're going to want their paths done too, aren't they?'

'Well, why not?' Connor grinned. 'I thought you were supposed to be the fittest Scout in Tiger Patrol.'

'I am too,' replied Abby, putting the shovel over her shoulder and leading the way to the next job. 'I'll do this one, and you do that one over there. I bet I'm finished before you!'

'Dead heat!' announced Toby as Connor and Abby finished their paths. 'Now let's see Jay against Priya. I bet Priya's going to win.'

'No chance,' said Jay — and was astonished

when Priya finished a good five seconds before him.

'My path must have been wider,' he said in disbelief.

'Let's face it,' said Priya. 'Girls are just better than boys. That's all there is to it!' She exchanged high-fives with Abby.

'Hey, look,' said Andy suddenly. 'Who's that with Mrs Holmes?'

The old lady they had helped earlier had emerged from her front door and was coming down her path leaning on the arm of a tall, very suntanned young man.

Jay looked up. 'Oh, that's Danny,' he said. 'Mrs Holmes's grandson.'

He returned to his digging. The other Tigers were all staring at him in disbelief.

'But it's Danny Holmes,' Connor said at last. 'He plays for United. Why didn't you tell us his grandma lived in your street?'

'I never thought,' said Jay. 'You know I'm not into football.'

'But he's famous,' began Abby, then clamped her mouth shut when she saw that Danny Holmes was coming over to join them.

'Nice job you did on my gran's path,' he said, smiling. 'Can I give you a hand?'

Danny worked as hard as any of them, and soon the Scouts were chatting to him as if they'd known him all their lives. They were clearing their final path, and Connor was thinking that they should all be heading home, when he looked up and saw the two PCSOs coming down the street towards them. In front of them were Lee and Sean and Lee's little sister. When they got closer, Connor saw that the boys' trousers were soaking wet.

Barbara crossed the street to talk to them while Lee and Sean stared sullenly into the distance. Danny Holmes stood there watching, unnoticed by the two teenagers.

'We were in the nick of time,' Barbara told them. 'Those boys should be grateful to you lot. I don't know what would have happened if we hadn't arrived when we did.'

'Did they actually fall in?' asked Priya.

'They were jumping up and down on the ice. Luckily for them they were close to the edge and, like I said, we arrived in time to pull them out.'

'That pond's only about a metre deep,' Lee yelled angrily across the road. 'Anyone'd think you'd done some kind of big rescue. You should be out catching criminals. Or clearing old ladies' paths like these saddos.'

Abby suddenly flung her shovel on the ground and stormed across the road. 'The only saddos around here are you lot.' She stood in front of Lee with her hands on her hips, furious. 'You were happy enough to let us help you when Sean broke his arm, weren't you?'

'Huh,' Lee sneered. 'You think we needed you? We would have got back just fine on our own, but you had to butt in.'

'You are unbelievable,' said Abby. 'Sean had a broken arm and you didn't have a clue what to do. None of you did. You would have been stuck out on the moors all night, and no one would have known where you were.'

'Abby, forget it,' said Connor, putting a hand on her shoulder. Everything Abby was saying was true, but Lee obviously wasn't in the mood for listening – although Sean was looking at the ground and his face was red.

Abby shook Connor's hand off angrily. 'Someone has to tell them,' she said. 'What if your sister had fallen in?' she demanded. 'What then?'

The little girl was holding tightly to the woman officer's hand, hiding her face. 'Hayley's *my* sister, not yours,' Lee said angrily. 'You just leave us alone, OK? Keep away from us, or else.'

'Or else what?' began Abby, but now Andy came and stood in front of her with a glance at Connor.

'Come on, Abby,' he said quietly. 'What's the point?'

Abby shook her head and turned away. Lee darted another unpleasant look at her.

'I'm sorry, kids,' Barbara said. 'You can't help

some people. We'll take them home and have a word with their parents. Thanks for everything you've done.' She looked along the street. 'I see you've all been working hard.'

Lee gave a scornful laugh, but suddenly he found Danny Holmes standing in front of him. His jaw dropped as he realized who Danny was.

'Have you got anything else to say?' Danny asked him. 'Because I've been helping them to clear these paths. I thought maybe you'd like to have a go at me too. Well?'

As the two PCSOs hurried Lee and Sean away, Danny turned back to the Tigers. 'How did I do?' he said. 'Did you see the looks on their faces?' His face cracked into a broad grin, and suddenly they were all laughing. 'Come on,' he said. 'My gran's got some refreshments ready for us. I reckon we've earned them!'

Much later, when Danny had left and the Tigers were completely full of three different kinds of cake and large amounts of hot chocolate, they stood together in the road outside Mrs Holmes's house.

'How cool was that?' said Abby. 'We've been eating cake with a Premier League footballer.'

'And all because we cleared an old lady's path.' Connor grinned. 'Listen, I've got a plan for tomorrow. This is a perfect chance to learn how to build snow shelters. We really ought to know how to do it if they're going to call us the Survival Squad.'

'Great,' said Toby. 'I've got some plans for igloos at home. And I'll look on the internet.'

'We *are* going to do more skiing, aren't we?' said Abby.

'Of course,' said Connor. 'But now we'd better get home. Tomorrow's going to be a busy day.'

CHAPTER 5

The following morning Connor arrived in the park at the head of a small convoy. The Tigers had made their way through the streets on their cross-country skis, each following exactly in the track made by the leader, the last in the line pulling the two sledges tied together. It had been an incredibly tiring journey, and Connor could certainly understand why his dad had been out of breath the day before. He was just wondering where Abby and Andy were when he heard Jay's voice.

His friend was pointing up at the slope. 'Look!' he said. 'How cool is that?'

Connor turned his head and saw Andy skiing down towards him. 'What happened?' he said, confused. 'I missed it.'

'Andy did a complete three-sixty in the air,' said Toby. 'Look, here comes Abby.'

All the Tigers turned to watch. 'She hasn't landed one yet,' Andy told them as he joined them. 'We've been here for hours. Abby woke me up while it was still dark! We've been using that bump there to get air. Here she goes!'

Abby hit the bump at speed, and took off. 'Too fast,' said Andy. 'And she's got too much rotation.'

She landed in an explosion of snow, out of which a single ski came flying into the air. 'Abby!' yelled Andy, running towards her. 'Are you OK?'

But somehow Abby was still upright. She came gliding across the snow on one ski, punching the air in triumph. 'I landed it,' she yelled at Andy. 'I told you I would!'

'That was awesome,' said Priya. 'I don't know how you managed to keep going.'

'Well, actually,' replied Abby, with a glance at Andy, 'it was a pretty rubbish landing. I have to admit, Andy is the expert at jumps and tricks.'

'But Abby's the one for downhill stuff,' Andy said, flashing a quick grin at his friend. 'Take a look at this.'

The Tigers gathered round, and Andy showed them some video of Abby flashing down the hill in a series of incredibly tight turns.

'That's unbelievable,' exclaimed Connor, admiring her talent. 'You look like a professional!'

'Actually, they're called short-radius turns,' Abby said, looking very pleased at Connor's praise. 'It feels pretty scary when you first start to do them.'

'And you fall over a lot,' laughed Andy. 'At least, you do if you're Abby. Take a look at this!'

'Hey, what are you doing?' she demanded as he showed them video of her crashing to the ground again and again. 'I told you to delete that!'

'No, it's cool,' said Jay. 'It's like those skateboard DVDs. They always have a wipe-out section.' He sucked in his breath sharply as Abby crashed and rolled a final time on Andy's tiny screen. 'You're going to be covered in bruises!' he said. 'Can you show us how to do that stuff? Or maybe some of those trick jumps?'

Andy shook his head. 'I wish we could, but there's no way you can do that on those cross-country skis.'

'And I've done enough skiing for now,' added Connor. 'It's easy following someone's tracks, but it's incredibly hard breaking trail.'

'Even so,' said Toby, 'we could travel a long way like that if we all had the right equipment. I've been thinking – maybe we could go on an expedition to Ashmore Hill. It's only a couple of miles out of town.'

'That would be amazing!' said Abby. 'Ashmore Hill is huge. You could get a proper run downhill there. I don't think I can wait until Easter to do some real Alpine skiing again.' Then her face fell. 'But me and Andy haven't got cross-country skis. We'd have to walk.'

'I'll talk to my dad,' Connor said. 'I bet he'll

know a way we can get hold of some more. We ought to try and get them anyway, because then we could use them on the Search and Rescue exercise. It's definitely much faster than walking.'

The Tigers all nodded agreement. Only Evie, the second-in-command of the Search and Rescue team, had used cross-country skis before, so it would be great if they could demonstrate how useful they were.

'What about these shelters, then?' asked Toby. 'They could be important if we have to keep an injured person warm. I brought along a plan of how to build one.'

Connor looked at the piece of paper Toby handed him. 'It says we have to saw blocks out of the ice,' he said.

'I know.' Toby was apologetic. 'But we can make do by rolling up big snowballs, can't we?'

'It's worth a try,' said Connor. 'We'll split into two teams and have a competition. You have to build an igloo for the whole patrol. I'll be with Abby and Andy.'

Ten minutes later Connor's team had completed the first layer of wall and left a space for a door. It was hard work, and they stood there for a moment getting their breath back.

A small boy with spiky red hair, who had been watching them with his friends, came up to them. 'Hello, I'm Hamish,' he said. 'Can we help?' His mum was standing a little way away and she gave them a wave.

'Sure,' said Andy. 'All you have to do is make big snowballs the same size as those. Bring them over and we'll put them on the igloo.'

With lots of enthusiastic help, the igloo grew quickly. From time to time Connor glanced through the trees to see how the others were doing. It looked as if it was going to be a close-run thing.

'Won't the roof just fall in?' asked Abby as he and Andy completed another row of blocks and the little kids ran off to fetch more snow.

'I don't know.' The wall was nearly as high as Connor's head now, and it tilted towards the centre, leaving a circle of sky above their heads.

'I think a couple more rows will do it. About ten more snowballs,' he said, turning to Abby. 'I bet the others will say we cheated, getting those kids to help.'

'Who cares?' said Abby. 'It's going to be an amazing igloo. Let's get all the snowballs ready, then finish it together.'

They joined the little boys and helped them to make the final few snowballs, then rolled them back to the igloo.

'This is going to be the tricky bit,' Connor said. 'I think we have to put the last few blocks in from the inside. Hold on a sec.'

He pulled off his gloves with his teeth and extracted Toby's piece of paper from his pocket. 'It says here that the blocks will hold each other up,' he told the others, 'but we have to get them all in place first. You two might have to hold some up while I fit the last one in.'

They crawled in through the low doorway and the kids followed them inside. 'Hey,' said Abby, 'you're in the way.'

'No they're not,' said Andy. 'They're just the right size to clear all this loose snow out through the doorway. OK, Hamish?'

The redheaded boy grinned up at him and then set to work. Andy and Abby helped him while Connor shaped the top layer of snowballs, ready to take the final pieces of the jigsaw. When the floor was clear, Abby and Andy began pushing snowballs inside, and Connor fitted them into place one by one. Finally there was just a small opening left. Connor lifted a snowball into position, and Andy held it in place while Connor picked up the final one and jammed it into the hole. Then both of them slowly removed their hands, and Abby and the small boys cheered loudly.

Connor couldn't quite believe that the roof was staying up. It seemed like magic. Then he heard voices outside, and Toby, Jay and Priya crawled in through the entrance.

'Awesome,' said Toby. 'It's bigger than ours, but we finished first. Only this isn't finished – not really. You have to stuff all the cracks with snow. *And* you had help.'

'We'll do that,' said Hamish eagerly, and all the Tigers laughed.

'You see what I mean?' said Toby. 'But we don't care because we won anyway. Come and see our igloo.'

They all crawled outside, and the small boys began collecting snow to fill the cracks. Their mum came over and introduced herself. 'I'm Maggie Johnston,' she said. 'The redhead is mine. It's a magnificent igloo.'

'I think we'll have to make this lot honorary members of Tiger Patrol,' Connor said, looking at the boys with a smile.

They left Mrs Johnston helping the children, and walked over to admire the other igloo. It was smaller, as Toby had said, but his team had made a brilliant job of filling the cracks and smoothing out the surface. They all managed to squeeze inside, and Connor reluctantly admitted that Toby's team were the winners.

'But your igloo will be better for brewing up,' Toby said. 'I've got my stove in my rucksack, and some water, and plenty of instant hot chocolate. I bet those kids would like some.'

They all agreed that it was the best hot chocolate they had ever had, even though they were sitting with the roof of the igloo dripping on their heads.

When they had finished they all crawled out into the bright sunshine again and waved goodbye to Mrs Johnston and the children.

'I bet a snowhole wouldn't be half as good as that,' said Jay as Andy shot some footage of the outside of the igloo.

'No,' said Toby thoughtfully. 'But it would be much quicker to dig a hole, and can you imagine doing all that in a storm?'

'Uh-oh,' said Abby. 'We've got trouble.'

Connor turned and saw Lee and Sean marching purposefully towards the igloo.

'You think you can go around spoiling other people's fun, right?' said Lee.

'And you think it's OK to get the police onto us?' added Sean. 'Well, it's not!'

'They weren't the police,' said Connor. 'They were—'

'We know what they were,' said Lee. 'We were having a good time yesterday until you lot messed it up. So now we're going to pay you back, OK?'

'Oh, right,' said Abby angrily. 'So you didn't actually fall into the pond, then? You didn't have to be rescued?'

'Don't waste your time, Abby,' Connor said. 'Let's go back to the others.'

'That's right,' spat Lee. 'You tell her. You'd better shove off before we snap those stupid skis in half. Go on. Or maybe you should watch us smash this thing up first.'

He launched a kick at the wall of the igloo, and a large section crashed to the ground. He looked defiantly at the Scouts, daring them to challenge him. Connor felt the blood pounding at his temples. Lee was a bully, and Connor was sure that, like most bullies, he'd go to pieces if someone took him on. He took a step forward and felt Andy's hand on his arm.

'Don't,' said Andy quietly. 'We can just walk away, like you said. They won't bother us when we're all together.'

'OK.' Connor took a deep breath and turned away, ignoring Lee's mocking laughter. His heart was still pounding. 'You're right, Andy,' he said. 'But somehow I don't think we've seen the last of that lot.'

CHAPTER 6

More clear, sunny days and frosty, star-filled nights followed. Each evening after school, Andy and Abby spent time outside identifying constellations and discussing the coming Search and Rescue exercise and the expedition to Ashmore Hill.

'We *have* to get cross-country skis,' Abby said on Thursday night as they stood in her garden. Andy was trying to show her the stars that made up the head of Leo. 'Stop going on about stars and *think* of something.'

'I asked my dad to buy me some,' said Andy, flashing a torch on his star chart. 'He took one look at the price and then he just laughed.'

'My mum too,' said Abby despondently.

A door opened, and bright light spilled across

the garden. 'Connor's here,' her mum called.

Connor crunched across the snow with a canvas case in his hands. 'You're in luck,' he said. 'My grandparents went back to Manchester today and my grandpa left these for you, Abby. And there are his boots too. He said you should wear an extra pair of socks to make them fit.'

'But they're his own skis,' Abby said, lifting the flap to peer inside, then looking up at Connor. 'Are you sure he said I can use them?'

'Sure,' replied Connor. 'There's no snow at all in Manchester and he's really fed up he had to go back. He said he'd rather someone was using them.'

'But what about me?' said Andy gloomily. 'I'll be the only one without cross-country skis.'

'No, you won't,' replied Connor. 'There are two pairs in that bag. The others are my dad's. And his boots will fit you. I checked.'

'Awesome,' breathed Abby. 'Come on, Andy. We can try them out now. We have to be good enough to use them on the Search and Rescue exercise. We've only got tonight and tomorrow.'

'That's amazing,' said Andy, pulling on Dr Sutcliff's boots. 'They're a perfect fit. Tell your dad I don't know how to thank him, Connor.'

There wasn't a lot of space in Abby's garden, but that didn't stop her. She remembered the instructions Connor's grandpa had given her very clearly, and she set to work perfecting her technique. She barely noticed when first Connor and then Andy said goodnight.

'It's ten o'clock and you've got school in the morning,' her mum called eventually from the back door. 'You're going to wear a hole in the lawn.'

Abby took off the skis and brushed all the snow off them carefully before placing them in their bag. The idea of a long journey on skis had taken hold in her mind, and that night she dreamed of the endless snowfields of Norway until the alarm clock woke her for school.

When the Scouts' minibuses arrived at the country park the following Saturday morning,

Rob and Soraya from the Search and Rescue team were waiting for them. The first thing Rob did was to check that all the Scout patrols had the correct clothes and equipment. The Search and Rescue team were all dressed in orange waterproof jackets and trousers.

'You'll need gaiters if you're walking around in the snow,' Rob told them. 'We've brought some spares for anyone who doesn't have any. Have you all got gloves and hats and a hot drink? Good.' He turned to the Tigers and smiled. 'You seem to be better equipped than we are!'

The Tigers were standing holding their skis. 'You should be able to get through our first challenge quickly on those,' Rob said. 'So we'll send you out first while Soraya takes the other Scouts down to the Conference Centre. Come with me, Tigers.'

He led them uphill from the car park. Abby remembered that there had been grassy hills here, stretching off towards the distant river, but now everything was smooth and white.

Rob was handing postcard-sized sections of map to Connor and Toby. 'This is a combination of a navigation exercise and some first aid,' he said. 'I've marked the position of a casualty on the map. Your job is to find them and work out what's wrong with them. OK?'

'Who are the casualties?' asked Jay.

'That'll be Pete, the tall guy, and Evie – remember her? She's a nurse, so she'll soon tell you if you can't work out what's wrong with her! Find them quickly or they really will start getting cold.'

Toby, Andy and Abby were working in one team; they were searching for Pete. Toby inspected the map carefully.

'What are you doing,' demanded Abby. 'The others have already started – look!' She pointed at Connor, Jay and Priya, who were already setting off to search for Evie.

'I know,' Toby replied, 'but there's a lot to think about. We have to know how fast we're going to travel on these skis. We can't count our steps, can we? So how are we going to know how far we've gone?'

'I know!' said Abby. 'Hang on.' She removed her boots from her skis and set off across the snow.

'What are you doing?' called Andy. 'Stop!'

Abby ignored him and kept going. Finally she turned and faced the other two. 'This is a hundred metres,' she called. 'I counted and added ten per cent because this snow is hard going. Now you two ski to me and we'll time you. Then we'll have some idea how long it takes to ski a hundred metres.'

'Genius!' Toby was already setting his stop-watch. 'Go, Andy!'

Andy set off, breaking trail, and Toby followed in his tracks.

'Two minutes,' announced Toby as Andy tried to catch his breath. 'That's slow. Slower than walking.'

'You see if you can go faster, then,' grunted Andy. 'I was doing my best.'

'I'm not complaining,' said Toby. 'Let me just work this out. We have to assume we'll do a bit less than three kph. Our casualty is one point five kilometres from here as the crow flies, but I think we should stay on the level and not go over that hill.'

'Too right,' agreed Andy.

'Well, then,' said Toby, measuring with the edge of his compass, 'we'll go one point five kilometres on a bearing of twenty-three degrees and then five hundred metres on a bearing of three hundred degrees. Everyone agreed?'

'OK,' said Abby, looking at the map. 'But isn't one point five kilometres too far to go on one leg of the journey?'

'Good thinking.' Toby consulted the map again. 'In about four hundred metres the land on our left should start to rise – look at these contours. We'll aim for that point. It should take about eight minutes. I'll lead the first leg. You go at the back, Andy, and check that I'm on the right bearing.'

'I don't think the others did all this,' said Abby.

'They might be lucky,' Toby replied. 'But then again, they might not. I reckon you can't be too careful. We'll show them how it's done.'

Meanwhile Connor was following Jay and Priya up a very gentle slope. It had been Jay who had spotted the clue that had enabled them to set off so quickly. 'The casualty is on the far side of that stream,' he said. 'If we head in that direction we can't possibly miss the stream. Then we follow it and find them. No trouble.'

It seemed like a great idea, and Jay was keen to break trail. Skiing along in his tracks was smooth and relatively easy. He tried to do all the things his grandpa had told them about skiing uphill: keeping his weight low and forward, transferring all his weight from one ski to the other. He could see that Jay and Priya were doing the same things, and doing them well.

He paused for a moment to check the bearing.

Jay was a little off course but, as he'd pointed out, they were bound to hit the stream. Connor skied on quickly to catch up with the others.

The slope ended and Priya took over the lead, digging the baskets on the ends of her poles into the snow and pushing herself onwards. They crossed a wide flat area, and then climbed gently once more. Priya paused and crouched down for a moment, gasping for breath. 'Go on, Connor,' she said. 'This is tough. It must be your turn.'

Connor moved past her and carried on. 'How much further, do you think?' he called back to Priya.

'Don't know,' she said. 'It must be quite soon, though.'

Connor pressed on, trying to ignore the burning sensation in his thighs. And now it was easier. The snow had flattened out and it wasn't so deep. 'Hey! This is good,' he called back to the others. 'I'm really moving. I—'

He stopped talking. Suddenly he needed all his concentration because the slope had steepened and the surface under his skis felt unreliable. He was moving faster than he wanted to move and he didn't like the sensation. The hillside steepened further, and now he was definitely travelling too fast. He heard Priya's voice from behind him:

'Connor! Stop! I don't like this!'

Connor desperately tried to remember what his grandpa had said about stopping. Something about a snowplough. Point the skis together. He turned his knees inwards, and suddenly he was tumbling to the ground. His face scraped across a patch of ice and he skidded to a halt. He saw Priya coming towards him down the slope and he reached out and grabbed her, pulling her to the ground beside him. Behind her, Jay somehow managed to get his skis into a snowplough and edge to an uncertain halt.

'This is all wrong,' said Jay. 'That's the river down there, not a little stream. We shouldn't be on a hill as steep as this. What's going on?'

Connor pulled the map out of his pocket. It

was obvious at once that they had come too far. Priya was the first to realize what had happened. 'The stream,' she said. 'We never saw it because it was frozen and covered with snow.'

They all stared at each other. 'We're going to look like idiots,' Jay said. 'I'm sorry, Connor. I messed up.'

'We all did,' said Connor, who was impressed by the way Jay was offering to take the blame. 'It wasn't just you. Look, if we find Evie it'll all be OK. We have to get back up that hill as fast as we can. OK, everyone? Let's go.'

CHAPTER 7

Toby, Abby and Andy had almost reached their destination. Abby was skiing in the lead, pushing on as fast as she could. 'Slow down a bit,' called Toby from behind her. 'If you go too fast, we might overshoot.'

'I can't help it if I'm fit,' grunted Abby. But she slowed down all the same. 'Shouldn't I be able to see Pete by now?'

'Yes, I think so,' Toby called back. 'Keep going for another minute.'

They halted together at the head of a small valley and Toby consulted the map. 'This is definitely correct,' he said. 'The land goes up on both sides and in front of us. We're facing north-west. There really isn't anywhere else on the map that looks like this.'

'So where's the casualty?' asked Abby.

'Maybe he's hidden?' suggested Andy. 'That Pete was a bit of a joker. He might have made a snow hole or something, just to confuse us.'

'We're going to have to search,' said Toby slowly. 'Even if we were standing exactly on the spot the grid reference refers to, we'd still have a hundred-metre square to search.'

'I thought a grid reference was a point on the map,' said Abby.

Toby shook his head. 'A grid reference gives you the corner of a square. Look – I've got it written in my notebook.'

'Save it for later,' interrupted Andy. 'Why don't we spread out and walk in a line until we hit the slope? That's how we found Jay, remember, when he was lost in the woods. And we should call out. That's what you'd do if you were looking for a real casualty.'

Abby remembered their desperate search when Jay had gone missing on the moors. This was more straightforward. It was just an exercise, after all, she thought as they began to move slowly across the snow, keeping their eyes peeled for anything unusual, calling out Pete's name as they went.

'Nothing,' said Andy when they reached the end of the shallow valley. 'And you know what, no one's been here either. Ours are the only tracks.'

'OK,' said Toby. 'So what do we do now?'

'You're absolutely sure this is the right place?' Abby said.

Toby nodded. 'We have to think,' he said. 'It's possible that Pete has had a real accident on the way here. I mean, it seems like the most likely thing, doesn't it?'

'We have to work out how he would have got here.' The idea came to Abby in a flash. 'Here – give me the map, Toby. He wouldn't have come the same way as us. It would have left a trail and been a dead giveaway. But what's that, there?' She stabbed her finger at the map.

'It's a track,' said Toby. 'It runs from behind the

Conference Centre and passes a few hundred metres over there.'

'They probably dropped Pete off in a four-by-four,' said Abby. 'We should go straight up that slope there and take a look.'

'OK,' agreed Toby. 'But first I want to put a marker to show that we found the spot where he should have been. We did a really good job and it would be a shame if we couldn't prove it.'

He skied quickly back to the place where they had started the search, took off his skis, and started moving backwards and forwards in the snow.

'What's he doing?' demanded Andy impatiently, but Abby began to laugh.

'He's scraping our initials in the snow. Great idea, Toby,' she called out as he headed back towards them. 'Now show us the best way to get up this slope.'

'Right,' said Toby, concentrating. 'You kind of go sideways and just step upwards.' He demonstrated, and the others followed suit. It was hard work, but they didn't have far to go.

Toby reached the top first, and immediately gave a yell. 'I can see something. Hurry!'

Abby hauled herself up beside him. The ground fell gently away towards a track that bordered the woods. Halfway down the slope there was a flash of orange. 'Pete?' she yelled. 'Is that you?'

There was a faint answering cry. 'Come on, Toby,' she said. 'What are you waiting for? Follow in my tracks.'

She thrust herself forward through the snow. 'It's OK, Pete,' she called. 'We're coming.'

Pete was lying on his back, half in, half out of a black hole in the snow. His face was pale beneath the stubble of his beard. 'Am I glad to see you guys,' he said, then winced with pain. 'I can't believe I came out without a radio or a phone. And we're only a couple of hundred metres from the road.'

'What happened?' asked Abby. 'You're hurt.'

'I think I might have broken my ankle,' Pete

said through gritted teeth. 'There's a bench under here. The snow must have drifted over it. I had no idea it was so deep, and my foot went straight through. I think it's trapped in the bench somehow. What are the odds against that happening?'

'OK,' said Toby. 'One of us will stay with you. It had better be me, I think. Abby, you and Andy ski back to the Conference Centre and get help.'

'Aren't you cold?' Abby asked Pete. 'You look cold. I've got a hot drink in my flask.'

Toby shook his head. 'He can't have anything to eat or drink,' he told her. 'If he needs an operation, that would delay it. I've got a space-blanket in my rucksack. You go and get help.'

'He's right,' Pete said. 'If I could just pull myself out of here—'

'Don't,' said Toby. 'You might make it worse, and they'll be back soon with help.'

They left Toby unfolding the silver space-blanket, and moments later they reached the track. 'We can ski in the tyre tracks,' Abby said. 'Much quicker.'

It only took a few minutes to reach the Conference Centre; they found Rob waiting outside the door, looking at his watch. 'I was getting worried,' he said, then paused. 'But where's Pete?'

'Rob,' said Abby urgently. She had a stitch in her side and she was breathing hard. 'Pete's had a real accident. He thinks he's broken his ankle. Toby's with him.'

Rob's eyes widened. 'Get those skis off and jump in,' he said, running to the four–by-four. 'You'll have to show me. How did you find him?'

'He wasn't at the map reference,' Andy said as they drove back down the track. 'So we worked out where he must have been coming from. We thought we should check, just in case something had happened— Stop! This is it.'

'I can see why they call you the Survival Squad,' Rob said, opening the back of the four–by-four and removing a stretcher. 'We'll see if we can do this on our own. Otherwise I'll call for backup. Which way do we go?'

'Up here,' said Andy, setting off uphill through the deep snow.

'Wow!' said Abby, helping Rob with the stretcher. 'I thought it was hard work on skis, but this is ten times worse! Look – there they are.'

She pointed to where Toby was standing waving his arms. Beside him was Pete, in exactly the same position as when they'd left him.

When they reached the scene of the accident, Rob took a torch from his pocket and knelt beside Pete, clearing the snow away. He looked down into the hole in the snow. 'You've got your foot caught between the slats of the bench,' he said. 'I'll get a crowbar from the wagon and I reckon we can have you out of there. How come you didn't call in?'

Pete shook his head ruefully. 'I didn't bother to take a radio,' he said. 'I didn't think I'd need it.'

'OK,' said Rob when he returned. 'I'm going

to lever those bars apart, and Toby and Andy, you can pull him up. One . . . two . . . three . . . *now!*'

Pete groaned as they pulled him out and laid him down on the snow. 'Is it just the ankle?' Rob asked him, and Pete nodded.

'It feels better now that it's out of there,' he said.

'Well, you're going on the stretcher anyway,' Rob told him. 'There's four of us. One on each corner. Pete, you can hold Toby's skis. Seems like you were taking the job too seriously, mate. You were supposed to be a fake casualty, not a real one!'

Connor, Priya and Jay reached the top of the hill safely and looked out over the white landscape. 'There's absolutely no sign of the stream,' Priya said.

'But we know where it must be.' Jay was leaning over Connor's shoulder, scrutinizing the map. 'It's right in the middle of this flat bit, and just after where our casualty is meant to be there's a short steep bit. We can make for the middle and head north. If we start going down steeply we'll know we've gone too far.'

'And we can watch out for Evie as we go,' said Priya happily. 'I bet we'll find her really fast now. I'll go in front.'

Connor followed behind Jay. It felt good to be working as a team, everyone chipping in with ideas. Jay and Priya were the newest recruits to Tiger Patrol, but Connor realized that he would feel happy to be with either of them in a difficult situation. They halted roughly where Connor thought the stream must be, and he checked the bearing on his compass. 'OK,' he told Jay, who was taking over in the lead. 'There's a hill over there with a church on top of it. Just head towards that.'

Jay set off, but they had only gone about a hundred metres when Priya called out, 'I can see something! Over there!'

Connor saw Evie's orange jacket almost before he heard Priya's yell. Jay shifted course, and seconds later they were standing beside her.

'Hi, Evie,' said Priya. 'We found you!'

Evie just stared straight ahead. Her hat was lying in the snow beside her and she was shivering.

Connor remembered what Rob had said: *Treat it as if it was real. You have to find out what's wrong with them, but check for danger first.* He looked all around, but there was no danger that he could see. 'Can you hear me, Evie?' he said. 'Can you tell me what's the matter?'

Evie looked up, but she hardly seemed to recognize him. Connor knelt down beside her. There was no sign of any blood on her head – he wasn't sure how realistic they would make any injuries. Then he checked Evie's arms and legs, but there didn't seem to be anything wrong. 'I think this is hypothermia,' he said to the others, and they nodded their agreement.

Priya picked up Evie's hat and put it on her head while Jay took a plastic sheet out of his rucksack.

'You're going to be OK, Evie,' Connor said, feeling a little self-conscious, but determined to do a good job. 'I've got a spare jacket here, and you should have a drink from my flask. Here—'

A radio suddenly crackled in Evie's pocket. '*Base to Evie . . . Base to Evie . . . Have you been rescued yet? . . . Over . . .*'

Evie grinned and sat up, taking the radio out of her jacket. 'Evie to base . . . Rescued, diagnosed and treated . . . Back in ten minutes . . . Over and out.'

She put the radio away and stood up, brushing the snow off her trousers. 'Good work, you guys. I saw you go over there, and I was wondering if you'd figure out where you went wrong. Let's get back. You can tell me about it on the way. There should be some sandwiches and hot chocolate waiting for us – I really need something after lying out here in the snow.'

On the way back to base the Scouts quizzed Evie about Search and Rescue. It turned out she'd actually been a member of a Mountain

Rescue team in the north, and she enjoyed telling them about the foolish things people did to get into trouble on mountains. 'Those skis are terrific,' she said. 'I went on a course once, but then I moved down here. You're lucky to have them. Hey! What's Rob doing? Wait a minute. Those are your friends.'

Evie broke into a run, and they arrived to find Pete grinning up at them from a stretcher. 'Our casualty was a real one,' Toby told them.

'And they did all the right things,' said Pete. 'I'll tell you what, Rob. It's a shame they have to be eighteen. I'd have this lot on the team any time.'

CHAPTER 8

'I don't know how you do it,' Sajiv said to Abby as they watched Rob drive off to the hospital with Pete to get his ankle checked out. 'Every activity you do, something happens to you lot.'

The Panthers were waiting, impatient to start their exercise. 'It's because we're the best, obviously,' Abby replied.

'She's winding you up, Sajiv,' Toby interrupted. 'It was just bad luck that Pete walked over the bench. It could have happened to anyone.'

'It wasn't luck that we found him,' insisted Abby. 'It was quick thinking and excellent navigation.'

Julie approached them across the car park. 'Your turn now,' she told the waiting Panthers.

'Rob's left me in charge. Here are your maps. You start over here. Follow me.'

'Good luck, Sajiv,' Abby called after them. 'Don't—'

'Yeah, all right, Abby.' Connor had come up behind her. 'You wait – I bet there's something the Panthers are better at than us.'

Abby bit her lip. She was annoyed with herself. She was so used to joking with Andy that she sometimes forgot that not everyone had his sense of humour.

'It's the skis, isn't it?' said Priya as they watched the Panthers heading off through the snow. 'They're jealous of our skis.'

'*I'm* jealous of the skis,' laughed Julie, rejoining them. She was bundled up in a red puffa jacket and had a brightly patterned hat pulled down over her ears. 'But there's no need for anyone to be jealous,' she continued. 'Come and see what we've arranged for later on.'

Julie led the way round the back of the Conference Centre, and they saw the rest of the Troop busy clearing snow from a wide flat expanse that stretched away into the distance.

'Snow clearing!' said Jay. 'Not again! Do we have to? What is it, anyway? Another car park or something?'

'No.' Priya turned to the others, her eyes wide. 'It's ice, isn't it? It's for skating.'

'Got it in one!' said Rick. He was walking towards them accompanied by a man in a suit. They were both smiling. 'This is Greg Norris, the manager of the country park. That's an area of water-meadow that was flooded before the freeze. It's only about ten centimetres deep and it's perfect for skating. We agreed that if you lot would clear it, Greg would be happy for you to skate on it.'

'But we don't have any skates,' said Priya.

'Oh yes we do,' said Greg. 'From tomorrow we'll be hiring them out. The ads are going out on local radio today. We were worried we wouldn't get the ice clear in time, but you've solved that problem for us. So as soon as the job's done you can have a go.'

'What are we waiting for?' exclaimed Jay. 'Let's get on with it.'

By the middle of the afternoon the ice was completely clear of snow. All the Scouts had completed their Search and Rescue missions, and Sajiv came back looking very pleased after finding his casualty in record time. Greg Norris had laid on more drinks and biscuits for the Scouts. When they'd finished eating and drinking, they were taken to fetch ice skates from a tent that had been set up on the grass beside the ice. The light of the short winter afternoon was starting to fade, but as the Scouts emerged from the tent, Greg threw a switch and four floodlights lit up the scene.

Minutes later the ice was full of screaming, yelling Scouts, most of them moving very uncertainly across the surface.

'It's no good,' Connor said to Toby after he'd

been on the ice for ten minutes. 'My ankles are burning. It's really hard work just standing up. I can't seem to go forwards at all.'

'Me neither,' said Toby. 'But look at Priya!'

Priya shot past them, and then somehow turned and skidded to a halt in a shower of ice crystals.

Toby grimaced. 'You've done this before, haven't you?'

'We used to live in London,' Priya said, 'close to a big ice rink. I'll help you, if you like.'

'Not right now,' Connor said. 'I'm going to sit down for a bit. But maybe you should help Abby. I thought she'd be good at this as she's such a good skier. Aargh! I can't watch!'

On the far side of the ice, Abby's feet slid out from under her for the twentieth time. She sat down hard and banged the ice with her fist.

'Here,' offered Andy, skating up. 'Grab my hand. I'll pull you up.'

'I've had enough,' she said. 'I'll never be able to do this.'

Abby had been sure that skating would be easy – Andy didn't seem to be having any trouble. She grabbed his hand and pulled herself upright.

'Have one more go,' Andy said, 'but don't . . .'

'What?' demanded Abby.

'Just go a bit slower. You always try to do things too fast, you know you do.'

'I don't. And even if I do, it's only because I'm good at things. You don't moan when I ski fast.'

'Have you forgotten that time when you were learning?'

'I was only four then,' Abby said. But she felt herself blushing. She had skied off down a slope on her own, and had luckily collided with a snowdrift before anything worse could happen. It was the only time she could remember her dad being cross with her, but she'd felt as if she was flying. Skating wasn't like that at all.

Sajiv glided past. He was a little wobbly, but he had time to grin at Abby. 'At last!' he said. 'Something the Panthers can do better than you.'

Suddenly his feet slid from under him and he

crashed to the ground. He got up laughing and skated away.

'Let me help,' said Priya, skidding neatly to a halt beside Abby. 'Here, hold both my hands.'

Abby gripped them tightly.

'That's it. Now point your toes slightly outwards and lift one foot up just a tiny bit, then put it down again. Then the other foot. Take tiny little steps and don't try to slide. Keep your weight forward, just like you told us when we were skiing.'

'Hey, wait a minute,' said Abby. 'You're going backwards. How are you doing that? You don't seem to be moving anything.'

'Don't worry about me. Are you feeling more comfortable now?'

Abby nodded.

'I told you,' Andy said as he skated past. 'You were going too fast.' He turned to look at her and nearly fell over.

Priya laughed. 'You'll soon be able to skate much better than him. I can tell. Now, you're starting to move forward on your own, so try and keep your weight just a little bit longer on each foot. That's great. Now I'm going to let go of your hands. That's it! You're skating!'

Abby moved forwards, first on one foot, then the other. 'It's all about the edges,' she said, leaning her weight to one side and feeling the edge of her skate grip the ice. 'It *is* like skiing!' She pushed onto the other foot and felt herself glide faster. Then she switched feet again and—

'Hey, Abby, watch out!'

She looked up and saw Jay heading towards her, a look of panic on his face. But Priya somehow caught her by the arm and spun her out of the way.

'You know what?' said Priya. 'I think I'd better show you how to stop.'

Priya and Abby kept on skating long after everyone else had given up. Abby hardly even noticed that Rick, Julie and some of the country park workers had produced barbecues from somewhere. They hardly noticed the smell of burgers and sausages either.

'Hey, you two,' yelled Connor at last, through a mouthful of burger. 'Come and get some food. You're not in training for the Olympics, you know. And look, Pete's back!'

Sure enough, Pete was standing at the edge of the ice, leaning on a pair of crutches and waving at them. 'It's just a sprain, luckily,' he told them as they sat on chairs and began to remove their skates. 'It looks like you've had a busy afternoon.'

Abby put on her shoes and stood up. She felt as if her feet were stuck to the ground, and her muscles were starting to burn and stiffen.

Priya grinned. 'You're going to be sore.'

'But I can skate,' Abby said. 'Or I nearly can. Thanks, Priya.'

They walked over to join the others. 'It wouldn't be the Olympics anyway,' Toby was saying to Connor. 'It would be the *Winter* Olympics.'

'Funny you should say that, Toby,' said Rick,

handing burgers to Abby and Priya. 'I've been talking to the leaders of the other Troops in town. If this weather lasts, we're thinking that we might have a Winter Sports Day of our own. They say it's going to stay cold, and there will be more snow too. So next Saturday could be the big day.'

'You mean, we'll have races and ice skating, with judges giving marks?' asked Connor.

'Something like that,' said Rick. 'I've had a word with Greg Norris and he's happy to host the event here. You've really helped him out today. It should be a lot of fun. Each Troop can represent a country that's good at Winter Sports. I just need a volunteer to plan everything out on a computer.'

'Me and Jay could do that,' offered Toby. 'Couldn't we, Jay?'

'Sure,' said Jay. 'But we'll need all the info.'

'It's here.' Julie tapped a folder lying on the table. 'I've been jotting down some ideas, and as soon as we have a list of competitors I'll email it to you. We'll have skating races, speed trials on toboggans and a downhill ski course. We'll give points for complete beginners too. Anyone who skis or sledges or skates can earn points, and I think we might have some snowboarders too. Can you really manage to make a timetable out of all this?'

'No problem,' said Jay. 'We can start on it as soon as we have the details – right, Toby?'

'OK,' said Rick. 'Now, while we're all here, I think Rob wants to say something to you.'

'You've all done really well today,' Rob told them. 'You all found your casualties and no one killed them with the wrong treatment – not even our real casualty.'

There was laughter at this and Pete gave them a wave.

'We never expected to end up ice-skating today,' Rob continued, 'and before we go I want to give you a warning about frozen ponds and rivers. I know some of you have already reported an incident, and you can understand how tempting it is to venture onto the ice. All I can say is, *don't do it*! And you should all remember a basic rule of Search and Rescue – your first duty is to look after your *own* health and safety.'

'My dad says health and safety is a joke,' Jay called out.

'Plenty of people think that,' Rob replied. 'But you wouldn't believe how often people die jumping into rivers trying to rescue someone else. If you see that someone's gone through the ice, please don't go after them. Call nine-nine-nine and try to get a lifebelt to them, or a ladder, or something that will reach out over the ice.'

Abby glanced around at the serious faces of the other Scouts. It had been a great day, but Rob had just reminded them that Search and Rescue was often a matter of life and death.

'OK,' said Rob. 'I see you've got the message. I can tell you that this ice is perfectly safe, so why don't you all enjoy yourselves. With any luck we'll see you at your Winter Sports Day!'

CHAPTER 9

On Sunday night Connor was closing his
bedroom curtains when he saw snowflakes
drifting by. At three in the morning he was wide
awake. He went to the window and saw snow
falling thickly outside, piling up on the
windowsill. He finally drifted off to sleep – only
for his mum to wake him when it was still dark,
the phone in her hand.

'This girl is impossible,' she said, 'but I suppose
you'd better get up. It looks like you're going on
your expedition!'

It was Abby on the phone. 'The schools are
closed, Connor! Every single one! There's tons
and tons of snow out there. We'll have Ashmore
Hill to ourselves. It'll be perfect practice for the
Sports Day, and if you lot have sixteen hours on

skis you'll be halfway to your Snowsports Badges.'

'OK.' Connor felt nearly as excited as Abby sounded. 'You call Andy and Toby and I'll call Jay and Priya. We'll meet at Priya's house at eight-thirty.'

Connor dressed quickly, putting on plenty of layers. His rucksack was already packed and waiting by the door.

'Keep to the side roads until you get out of town,' his dad advised him as Connor gulped down his porridge. 'There won't be any traffic. We've had about fifteen centimetres of fresh snow and the police are telling people not to go out in their cars. I'd come with you given half a chance. Unfortunately people don't stop getting ill when it snows. I bet I'll have a full surgery.'

'Tough luck,' Connor said. 'We'll be back before dark.'

'Make sure you are,' his dad replied. 'I've told all the other parents that they can depend on you.'

'You talked to them?'

'Of course I did. We all want you to take on challenges. That's why you joined the Scouts, after all. But you have to remember that Priya and Jay haven't been Scouts for very long. Their parents just wanted to check that I thought this expedition was safe, and I told them it was, OK? I'm sure you'll have a great time. You'd better get moving. It won't do to keep young Abby waiting!'

When Connor reached Priya's house, all the Tigers were waiting outside. He looked around at them approvingly. They looked like a proper expedition in their windproof jackets and gloves and hats, the sledges neatly packed. Toby's sledge was loaded with bulging bags.

'How come everyone else has one rucksack, but you have three!' Connor asked.

Toby looked back at him for a moment, his green eyes serious in his dark face. 'It's all useful stuff in there,' he said, patting the bags and checking the straps. Then he looked up and grinned. 'You know you'll be glad I've brought it.'

'Well, just don't ask me to pull your sledge,' said Connor, but he couldn't help smiling. 'Is everyone ready?'

Jay and Andy had been sharing Andy's headphones, listening to a track on his iPod. They took out the headphones and Andy stowed the iPod away.

'We've been here for ages,' replied Abby, pulling off her hat and rearranging her hair in an unsuccessful attempt to keep it in place. 'Can we please get going now?'

Priya's parents waved them off as they headed down the street, with Abby breaking trail as fast as she could. They made good progress until they neared the edge of town.

'Hey, look,' called Andy, who had taken over the lead, 'there are real snowdrifts at the end of this street.'

The wind had sculpted the snow into a series of drifts that were nearly as tall as they were. Andy sidestepped up onto the top and pushed himself over, but when Abby tried to drag the sledge up, the nose buried itself instantly in the deep snow. They tugged at the rope, but only succeeded in forcing the sledge deeper into the drift. A short way off, Toby and Jay were trying the same thing, but all their efforts were useless.

'It's no good,' Andy said. 'We'll have to go round another way.'

'We need shovels,' Jay realized. 'Maybe we should go back and get one.'

'There's one in here.' Toby bent over his bags. 'I've just got to remember where it is.'

'I don't believe it,' said Connor, but the others just laughed as Toby extracted a shiny blue folding shovel and began heaving snow out of the way.

They took it in turns, and eventually they were able to put their skis on again and drag the sledges though the worst of the drifts.

'It's like being in the Antarctic,' said Toby. 'I've been reading about Captain Scott. They pulled their sledges over hundreds of miles of ice and snow, trying to get to the South Pole.'

'Only they don't have streets and houses in the Antarctic,' Andy pointed out.

'And Captain Scott didn't like skis,' Connor told them. 'He thought it was easier on foot. That's one of the reasons why Amundsen got to the Pole before him. Plus he didn't have teachers like my grandpa. Look, we're here. We're leaving civilization behind. Out there it's a wilderness!'

Ahead of them, the last row of houses came to an end and the open countryside began – but it was countryside that was very different from the one they were used to. The snow had blurred the edges of everything. Drifts had piled against the stone walls that edged the main road. A snowplough had been through, clearing a track that was wide enough for two cars to pass each other. Between the piles of snow thrown up by the plough and the invisible walls was a smooth area unmarked by any tracks except those of birds and small animals.

The Tigers skied in single file. The road

continued gently uphill for a while and then levelled out and curved round to the left.

'There it is,' said Connor as the rounded bulk of Ashmore Hill appeared in front of them.

They all stopped for a moment to look. They could see a few small figures climbing the slopes, and two or three sledges careering down them.

'Hardly anyone,' breathed Abby. 'This is going to be amazing.'

'Toby?' said Jay. 'What are you doing?'

Toby had lifted the cover off his sledge and was rooting around in a rucksack. 'I've had an idea. We can take a short cut. The snow's bound to have filled in this ditch.' He pointed to a fine blue line on his map. 'I bet we can ski right over the top of it. We can get away from this road and go straight across the fields.'

'Look at it!' cried Abby. 'Unexplored country! It's even better than the country park. New powder snow! This is what your grandpa was talking about, Connor. If you ski across that, you'll really deserve your Snowsports Badge.'

'OK,' said Connor. 'You're the expert, Abby. But how do we get into the field?'

'Look' – Priya pointed to a post sticking out of the snow – 'there's the top of the footpath sign, and there's a gap beside it.'

Toby checked his compass. 'We can head directly for that pine tree at the foot of the hill. It's a whole lot easier than navigating in the mist and rain.'

'You can say that again,' said Priya with a shudder.

'Don't worry,' laughed Abby. 'This is going to be fun. Ready, Andy?'

Abby set off across the snowfield. With each slide forward her skis sank several centimetres into the soft powder, so there wasn't really very much glide. She dug her poles into the snow on either side to give her support as she pushed herself forward. It was incredibly hard work, but she didn't mind that. This was a real adventure.

After a few more minutes she was forced to

stop, leaning on her poles and breathing hard. The surface of the snow glittered, the light refracted by millions of tiny crystals.

'My turn,' announced Jay, taking over the lead and battling on through the snow.

Abby grinned and followed behind him, enjoying the smoother ride in his tracks. 'You can't do this unless you work as a team,' she called back to Connor. 'No one could keep going in front for ever.'

'If anyone could, it would be you,' Connor called back, and Abby blushed, absurdly pleased at the compliment. One of these days, she thought, she would tell Connor what a great PL he was.

Fifteen minutes later they were approaching the foot of the hill. They could hear the shouts of the sledgers clearly now, echoing from the slopes ahead of them. 'Look' – Connor pointed to the left with his pole – 'there's the lake. It's completely frozen.'

'Where?' asked Priya. 'All I can see is snow.'

'By those birch trees,' Connor said. 'Where it's all flat. Look – there are ducks waddling around wondering where the water's gone.'

They all laughed. 'It would be a bit cold to swim in anyway,' said Andy, getting out his camcorder and aiming it at the ducks.

'It gives me the creeps,' said Priya. 'You could easily wander onto it and not know you were on the ice.'

'Don't worry,' Abby told her. 'We'd know how to rescue you. We've had training, remember? But we won't need that because we came here to ski. It's not much further now.'

She turned and headed up the gentle slope ahead of her. When she came over the brow, she saw a sledge hurtling towards her and moved swiftly out of the way, shouting a warning to the others. The sledge came to a halt in a snowdrift, throwing its occupants off into the snow. Three children and a woman in a stripy hat stood up laughing.

'Mrs Johnston!' said Abby, recognizing the

woman they had met in the park. 'How come you're here?'

'You were talking about this place, remember? Me and my friend Jean – Mrs Mitchell – thought it sounded like a good idea to bring the kids. Here she comes now.' She pointed towards another sledge rocketing down the steep slope. 'I expect you remember Hamish,' she continued. The red-headed boy grinned up at them.

'You must have got up early,' said Priya.

'We did,' replied Mrs Johnston, grabbing the rope of her sledge. 'Come on, kids. Back to the top.'

'We can leave our things over there,' Connor said. 'Away from where people are sledging.' He skied away for a hundred metres or so and chose a spot on a small hillock, then unclipped his skis and planted them in the ground. The others joined him and made a pile of bags and skis.

'Time for some real skiing,' said Abby, removing the cross-country skis and changing her boots.

'Don't let my grandpa hear you say that,'

Connor called after her as she led the way towards the hill, her skis over her shoulder. Andy followed close behind her. The others came behind with their sledges. Finally they all stood at the top, panting, looking out at the view.

A haze lay over the icy landscape, floating above the whiteness. Hedges and trees cast dark shadows on the snow. It was dazzling. At the bottom of the hill, the road was a dark line leading towards the town. Occasional cars moved slowly along it. As they watched, two of them pulled off the road. 'They'll get stuck,' said Abby.

'They're four-wheel drives,' said Toby, his binoculars to his eyes. 'It looks like they're coming sledging. I can see more people walking up the road.'

'We'd better get started, then,' said Abby. 'Before it gets crowded.'

'You're not really going to ski down that?' said Jay. 'It's kind of steep.'

Abby laughed. 'It's nothing,' she said. 'Ready, Andy?'

She took off down the hill. It was perfect. The edges of her skis bit into clean, new snow as she carved her first, perfect turn and prepared for a smooth transition into the next one. It wasn't a mountain, but it was still amazing. She imagined herself back in the Alps above Chamonix, flying down the Vallée Blanche. Then she saw a sledge coming across her path. The two boys yelled as they saw her, but she reacted instantly, throwing herself into a short radius turn, and then another, before continuing smoothly down the hill. She slewed to a halt in a fountain of snow, and Andy skied up beside her with a huge smile on his face.

'Great skiing,' he said. 'I could never have got out of their way like that. Let's do it again!'

As they climbed back up, they saw the others racing down on sledges. Toby and Jay reached the bottom first, tried to brake, and overturned, hurling themselves into deep snow. They stood up, brushing themselves down and laughing.

'You look like abominable snowmen!' yelled Abby, before trudging uphill again.

They spent a glorious two hours on the hillside. Gradually, more people began to arrive, but it was a wide slope and there was room for everyone. Then, as the Scouts all rested together at the top of the hill, Toby let out an exclamation.

'What is it?' asked Connor. 'What can you see?'

Toby was looking through his binoculars at the roadside where the cars were parked. 'I don't believe it,' he said. 'I can see Sean, and Lee, and two other boys. And Lee's got his little sister with him. They've got a big sledge. They're coming up here.'

'So what?' said Connor. 'We can easily keep out of their way. That lot won't bother to go further than they have to.'

The top of Ashmore Hill was a wide, rounded lump. The steeper slopes where they had been sledging and skiing faced south, towards the town, but now Connor was looking further west, where the hill fell away more gently towards a small valley.

'It's not as steep,' grumbled Abby. 'It won't be so much fun.'

'No, it's cool.' Andy pushed himself on a little further to get a better look into the valley. 'There are some great places to practise our jumps. Come on, Abby.'

The two friends skied on ahead. 'Watch,' called Andy, launching himself at a small hillock. 'I'm going for a backscratcher!'

Abby slewed to a halt and watched as Andy hit the top of the takeoff with his knees bent and his poles neatly by his side. She saw his skis come up behind him and he leaned back stylishly before making a clean landing. 'Come on,' he yelled. 'You try!'

The sledgers had stopped beside Abby. 'That was awesome,' Priya said, waving madly to Andy. 'Can you do that, Abby?'

'You bet. Just watch me!'

Abby flung herself down the hill. She was a confident jumper, but she'd never actually landed one of these. The takeoff came up fast. She crouched and tucked her poles in, and suddenly she was in the air. She felt herself turning. She tried desperately to keep her shape, but she was falling backwards. Her back hit the ground in a fountain of snow, and she slithered down to where Andy was waiting, skis all over the place.

Andy pulled her to her feet and she saw the camcorder in his hand. 'You didn't! Delete it, right now!'

'No way!' Andy laughed.

'Hey, Abby,' yelled Jay, running down to join them, taking enormous strides in the soft snow. 'That was spectacular!'

'Oh, no!' gasped Toby. 'Look at that!'

From where they stood they had a clear view back to the more popular slopes. They all turned to watch as a big sledge raced down the hill, straight towards two sledges loaded with children. Even from this distance Abby could see that Lee was steering it. She heard Mrs Mitchell cry, 'Watch out, kids! Get out of the way!'

Lee's sledge came hurtling down from above. It

missed the first group of children by a whisker, but their sledge turned over as they panicked. Lee plunged onwards, gathering speed all the time.

'It's all right,' breathed Abby. 'He's missed the other one too.'

But just as she was giving a relieved sigh, sure that they were safe, Lee slewed to the right and clipped the back end of the second children's sledge, flipping it over onto its side.

CHAPTER 10

'Come on,' said Connor grimly as they heard the screams of the children. 'They're going to need our help.'

When they arrived at the scene of the crash, they found several of the children crying and being comforted by Mrs Mitchell. Mrs Johnston was trying to disentangle Hamish from the wreckage of the sledge. The cord was hopelessly tangled in the broken slats and wrapped around the boy's leg. His trousers were torn, and blood was dripping from an ugly-looking gash in his knee.

'Can I help?' asked Connor.

'I can't get this rope off,' Mrs Johnston said. 'How could those boys be so stupid? It's only luck that one of these children wasn't seriously hurt.'

'I'm going to kill them,' said Hamish, grimacing with pain. 'I'm going to catch them, and I'm going to—'

'Be quiet, Hamish,' said Mrs Johnston. 'You'll do no such thing. Hamish is a bit of a hot-head,' she told Connor.

Connor grinned. He liked this little boy.

'Couldn't you cut the rope?' Priya asked him.

'Good idea,' replied Mrs Johnston. 'The sledge is useless now anyway.'

Connor shook his head. 'I'd rather not,' he said. 'I've got a spike in my knife that should help to get that knot undone. I'll just clear that broken wood out of the way first.'

The knife blade sliced easily through the protruding splinters. 'Great knife,' said Mrs Johnston. 'You keep it nice and sharp.'

'My grandpa says that a blunt knife is more dangerous than a sharp one,' Connor replied. 'This used to be his. He'll be glad it's been useful again. Now, let me get at the knot.'

It only took a few more seconds for him to

work the rope loose. Freed from the sledge, Hamish got slowly to his feet. Toby came over with a first-aid kit, and made him sit down on a rucksack. He looked carefully at the wound on Hamish's knee, then glanced up at Connor. He kept his voice calm, but Connor could tell that he had seen something that alarmed him.

He took a closer look at the little boy's knee, and realized at once why Toby was worried. A large splinter of wood was sticking out of the cut.

'Maybe you'd better take a look,' Toby said to Mrs Johnston.

'Oh, no! Let's see the Scouts in action,' she said. 'It's Toby, isn't it? You'd like Toby to repair your leg, wouldn't you, Hamish?'

The little boy nodded, and Toby knelt down beside him.

Connor took Mrs Johnston to one side. 'I didn't want to worry you,' he said, 'but I think that cut is quite bad, and there's a piece of wood still stuck in it.'

'But we can just pull it out and put a bandage on . . . can't we?' she said.

Toby stood up and left Priya to look after Hamish. 'We shouldn't do that,' he said quietly. 'I was talking to Pete about it while we were waiting for him to be rescued – Pete's a Search and Rescue expert,' he told Mrs Johnston. 'It's lucky I did because I know what to do. We have to call an ambulance. If we take it out it might make the bleeding much worse.'

'Oh dear,' said Mrs Johnston. 'Are you sure?'

'You really should call them now,' Toby said. 'Once I've put a bandage on, we can put him on a sledge and take him down to the car park.'

Connor looked around and saw that the other Tigers were helping Mrs Mitchell to cheer up the other children. Andy was filming the wreckage of the sledge, but he was having trouble because the kids kept pulling faces into the camera lens.

Mrs Johnston was talking into her phone. 'That's odd,' she said when she'd finished. 'The person I spoke to said to be sure and keep him

134

warm because we might have a bit of a wait. They say there's more snow on the way – but there's none here yet, is there?'

'But there is,' said Priya. 'Look!'

The first flakes of snow were already swirling around them. In the rush to deal with the accident, none of them had noticed the clouds that had rapidly covered the sky, blotting out the sun.

Toby was working carefully, placing pads of gauze on either side of Hamish's knee so that he could bandage it without putting pressure on the splinter of wood.

'Are we the only people left?' Connor asked Mrs Johnston. 'Where did everyone go?'

'They gave up when that lot arrived,' she replied, pointing to Lee and his friends, who were busy dragging their sledge back up the hill. 'They were probably sensible to go, but the kids were having such a great time, and so was I. Now look what's happened.'

'We should get ready to leave right now,'

Connor said. 'Let's get our stuff together while Toby's bandaging Hamish's knee.'

'OK,' said Mrs Johnston. 'I'm sure you're right. Kids! Come here, all of you.'

When they'd seen the snow falling, the children had started running around trying to catch snowflakes. It took the Scouts several minutes to round them all up and collect their cross-country skis and other gear, by which time the snow was falling more thickly and a breeze had sprung up, blowing it into Connor's face. He pulled up the hood of his jacket and then saw that Mrs Johnston was looking worried.

She was staring at the damaged sledge. 'I didn't think,' she said. 'The children are going to find it really hard to walk all that way. Mrs Mitchell and I pulled them on the sledges, and now there's only one that works.'

'It's OK,' Connor told her. 'Some of them can ride on ours. We can tie the broken sledge on top too. It'll be all right.'

The other Tigers began rearranging the loads

on their sledges so that the younger children could sit comfortably, but all the time the wind was rising and fine snow began to sting their faces. Connor took off his gloves to unfasten the straps on his sledge and found that his freezing fingers could hardly get a grip.

'Look,' said Abby suddenly. 'You can't see the road any more.'

'You can't even see the bench at the bottom of the hill there,' said Andy.

'I don't like this, Mummy,' said Mrs Mitchell's daughter, a little girl in a pink woolly hat with rabbit ears on it. 'I want to go home.'

Connor stood up and looked down the hill. Andy was right. It was getting very hard to see, and it would be nasty for the children sitting on the sledges. This fine snow would blow inside their clothes. They'd get very cold. 'This is no good,' he said. 'We should make a shelter and keep ourselves warm until the storm blows over. If we tip the sledges up on their sides, then we can get the little ones out of the wind.'

'I'd better check what's happening with the ambulance,' Mrs Johnston said, dialling rapidly.

She spoke briefly into the phone, then turned to Connor. 'They say they're sending a Search and Rescue team,' she told him. 'They want to know exactly where we are, and I'm not really sure.'

Toby pulled his map from his pocket. 'The grid reference is 467352,' he said, after double-checking his estimate. 'The south side of Ashmore Hill.'

Mrs Johnston repeated the information into the phone, and the Tigers unloaded their sledges again, and turned them on their sides. Toby sat Hamish on one of his bags and wrapped him in his spare fleece and then a silver space-blanket.

'Will they be able to find us?' Mrs Mitchell asked anxiously. 'It's getting awfully thick. How will they see?'

'They have GPS,' replied Toby. 'They'll find us all right, just as long as they can actually get here through the snow.'

The Scouts had soon made a wall that was just high enough to shelter the children, who crouched gratefully behind it.

'We could make it even better,' said Andy. 'We could get giant snowballs and build a proper wall like we did in the park. It'll keep us warm too, building it.'

'Good idea,' said Connor, starting to roll a snowball.

The others joined him. The snow had eased off just a little, but the wind was still blowing hard.

'Hey, Toby,' he said. 'Aren't you going to help?'

'I'm going to make hot chocolate,' Toby said, unwrapping one of the mysterious bundles that he had taken off his sledge. Connor looked over the top of the sledge wall to see what he was doing. 'I brought my stove,' Toby said, looking up with a smile. 'I thought it might—'

'Come in useful!' all the other Tigers chorused as Toby took out a silver bottle and filled the brass burner with fluid. He lit the fluid and a blue flame flickered. The small children gathered round to watch as he filled a pan with water from another bottle, placed it on the stove and covered it with a lid. 'You should keep clear,' he said. 'It's going to get hot, and you mustn't knock it over.'

Connor smiled. The children had formed a circle and were all watching Toby, wide-eyed and silent. Twenty minutes later the Tigers had made a rough semicircular wall of snow that sheltered everyone from the wind, and they were all sharing steaming cups of hot chocolate and nibbling on biscuits. Priya and Abby had even rigged up a roof using the plastic sheeting from one of the sledges fastened to a couple of ski poles.

'This is almost cosy,' said Mrs Johnston, although Connor could see that she was still anxious. 'I'm glad you're such a resourceful bunch. We would have been in a bit of a pickle if you hadn't known exactly what to do. Just look at that snow!'

Outside the shelter of the walls, thick snow was blasting past them horizontally. The wind was whipping it up off the ground too, so that the air seemed to be completely filled with swirling flakes.

'You can't see a thing,' said Connor, sticking his head round the end of a wall. 'You can't tell the difference between the land and the sky. It's a whiteout. It's lucky we didn't try and walk. We could have got totally lost. No – wait . . . I don't believe it!'

The snow had eased for a second, and Connor had caught just a glimpse of a dark shape flying down the hill. 'They're still sledging,' he said. 'They must be crazy. They haven't even got proper clothes. We should get them all in here.'

'We can't,' Abby pointed out. 'And anyway, they won't come.'

'Connor's right,' said Andy. 'We don't have any choice. Don't you remember? They've got that little girl with them. Lee's sister. I'm going to go and talk to them. I don't suppose they'll listen, but we have to try.' He pulled his hat down over his ears and began to put on his cross-country skis.

'Wait,' said Abby. 'You shouldn't do it on your own. I'm coming with you.'

'I don't think you should, Abby,' Connor said. 'You'll only get angry . . .'

'I won't say anything to them,' she said. 'Not a thing, I promise. But me and Andy know what we're doing in the snow. I'm the one who should go with him. You know I'm right.'

Connor hesitated, then nodded his agreement. He could see that Abby knew this was a serious situation, and she was right. She and Andy were the best equipped to deal with the snow. He just had to hope that conditions wouldn't get any worse.

'Hurry,' he urged them. 'There's no time to lose.'

Abby clipped her boots into her cross-country skis and stepped out of the shelter of the wall.

CHAPTER 11

Wind and snow blasted into Abby's face and rocked her backwards. For a moment she was blinded and found it hard to breathe. It was like diving into cold water. She staggered back into the shelter of the wall.

'It's wild out there!' she gasped. 'I can barely see through the snow.'

Andy and Connor exchanged worried glances. 'We'll all have to help. Get your skis on, everyone, this is serious,' Connor said. He put his head round the end of the shelter and drew it back quickly as a heavy squall of snow blinded him.

'We're going to need to be really careful,' he said to the other Tigers. 'You know what the Search and Rescue team told us. The first thing we have to do is make sure *we're* safe.'

'We'd better stay here, then,' said Jay. 'They're not going to do what we say anyway.'

Connor shook his head. 'They're in danger. We can't just leave them. We have to at least try, so here's what we'll do. We'll make a sort of human chain. Priya, you'd better go first. Ski in that direction and go as far as you can without losing site of the shelter. It won't be very far. Then you go next, Jay. Go past Priya and stop while you can still see her. Then the rest of us, one at time. Everybody ready? Make sure you can always see the person behind you. Let's go.'

Some of the small children complained when Priya left them, but Mrs Johnston and Mrs Mitchell quickly hushed them. Abby could see that the grown-ups were taking this just as seriously as they were.

The snow was thick and white and blinding. Connor went forward maybe ten metres with Priya, then called to Jay. Toby went out next, and then Connor left Priya and moved out past Toby and Jay, and then another few metres into the white storm of snow.

It was Abby's turn. She pulled her orange ski goggles over her eyes and moved off into the snow. She passed Priya, Jay and Toby and halted when she could just see Connor behind her. Andy came up beside her, his shape blurred by the snow, even though he was less than a metre away.

'This is hopeless,' he said, pointing into the whiteness. 'They were right over there.'

'We'll have to shout,' said Abby. 'It's the only thing we can do. You go ahead as far as you can . . . Lee!' she yelled. It felt very strange to be calling his name. 'Where are you? We're over here.'

She could hear Andy calling too, and Connor behind her, their voices strangely muffled by the snow. They all kept calling for what seemed like a long time. Eventually Abby stopped. She realized she was shivering.

'Abby,' came Connor's voice. 'That's enough. We have to go back.'

'OK,' called Abby, but then, as she turned to yell to Andy, she saw dark shapes stumbling towards her. 'Over here,' she called urgently. 'This way.'

The figures turned in Abby's direction. As they came closer, she saw that they were totally covered in snow. There were four of them. Lee was in the lead and he stared wildly at Abby.

'Andy,' she yelled. 'Come here. Hurry!'

Lee tried to speak. 'I d-d-d—' He was shivering so hard he couldn't get the words out. He was hugging himself and his teeth were chattering.

'What is it?' demanded Andy. 'What are you trying to say?'

'It's – it's – m-m-my s-s-sister Hayley. I . . . I d-d-d-don't know where she is. She's only s-s-seven . . .'

Abby saw the horror in Lee's face. She felt it herself. Somewhere out there in all this freezing snow there was a seven-year-old girl. She must be terrified. 'You have to get into the shelter,' she told Lee. 'You're freezing. It's over there.' She

146

pointed to where Connor was still waiting.

'I can't,' said Lee. 'I've got to find her.'

'We have to work out what to do first,' said Andy, taking hold of Lee's arm. 'We can't just go crashing around in this. It won't do any good.'

'Get off me!' Lee wrenched his arm away and took a couple of steps down the hillside. His feet sank deep into the snow and he fell over.

'He's right, Lee,' said Sean, sounding exhausted. 'You'll never find her on your own.'

Lee got to his feet and stood there for a moment before walking awkwardly after the others. Abby followed behind them, wishing that they would move more quickly. They passed the other Scouts one by one, and finally reached the shelter of the makeshift wall, where Connor insisted in knocking as much snow as he could off their clothes. 'It'll melt on you if you don't,' he said. 'And then you'll never get warm.'

Hamish recognized Lee at once, and anger flared in the little boy's face. 'You wrecked our sledge,' he yelled. 'You're mean.'

Mrs Johnston grabbed him from behind. 'You should all be ashamed of yourselves,' she began, looking at Lee and his friends, but then she saw Connor's face. 'What is it?' she asked him.

'It's Lee's little sister,' Abby said, her voice shaking. 'They don't know where she is.'

'All right,' replied Mrs Johnston. 'We should all stay calm. The Search and Rescue people are already on their way here. I'll find out what's happening.'

She took out her phone. After a few moments she spoke. 'Yes, that's right, I called earlier. Is there any news? . . . Yes, I know, but the situation has changed. A seven-year-old girl has gone missing in the storm . . . There must be *some* way you can get here . . . Yes, all right. I'll stay off the phone, but please hurry.'

She looked at the Scouts. 'This snow is so bad that none of the police or Search and Rescue vehicles can move right now. The road's blocked by abandoned vehicles and the helicopters are grounded. They'll send help as soon as they possibly can.'

They were all silent. They listened to the roar of the wind, and the plastic sheet flapped madly above their heads.

Abby knew they were all thinking about Hayley, alone out there, and terrified. 'Where did you see her last?' she asked Lee.

Lee shook his head. He was shivering uncontrollably, and the other boys didn't look much better.

'She was building a snowman,' said Sean suddenly. 'Down the bottom of the hill.'

'And you just left her there?' exclaimed Abby angrily.

'She was all right,' Sean replied. 'She was having a good time.'

'Here,' said Connor, throwing Sean his spare fleece. 'You'd better put this on. We'd better give them all our spare clothes,' he said to the others. 'And then we'll go and look for Hayley.'

'Not all of us,' said Abby. 'Me and Andy. We already talked about it, didn't we, Andy? We're strong skiers and we've got goggles, and our clothes are made for the mountains.' She felt a little scared by what she was saying, but she knew it was the right thing to do.

Connor thought for a moment. 'Toby should go too,' he said. 'He's the best skier of the rest of us, and with three of you moving in a line you'll have more chance of going straight. You'll have to be really careful. It won't do much good finding her if you can't get back here again.'

'We'll be able to get to the bottom of the hill all right,' said Toby. 'It's not that far.' He turned to Sean. 'Can you show me on the map where you saw her last?' he asked.

Lee was sitting beside Sean, a glazed look on his face, as if he wasn't really sure what was going on.

'It was about there,' Sean said, pointing. 'Near those trees.'

'OK,' said Toby, laying his watch on the map. 'I think we should go directly downhill first. That's a bearing of 193 degrees from here. But it's not going to be totally accurate. And then we'll work our way along the foot of the hill to the trees.'

'You have to add two degrees,' Jay pointed out. 'You forgot about the magnetic variation.'

'Right,' said Toby. 'Hey, Connor, can't Jay come too? He's the best navigator.'

'I was going to try to mend this sledge . . .' Jay indicated the broken mess they'd salvaged from the accident.

'I think three of you is enough,' Connor said. 'And it would be a big help to have an extra sledge. Do you really think you can fix that?' he asked Jay.

Jay looked thoughtful. 'I might need to borrow your knife. It's got a screwdriver in it, hasn't it?'

Connor took out the knife and handed it to him. 'My grandpa fixed a sledge with it once,' he said. 'In Norway.'

While Connor and Jay were talking, the others had been getting ready.

'I've set the bearing,' Toby said. 'It's actually only about two hundred metres to the bottom of the hill, but we'll still find it hard to go straight. You go first, Andy, then Abby, then I'll come last. I'll yell if you're going the wrong way. You've got a whistle, haven't you, Connor?' Connor nodded. 'When we find Hayley, we'll call Mrs Johnston and you can keep blowing the whistle. That'll help us find our way back.'

Abby pulled down her goggles and nodded to the others. Then they stepped out into the whiteness.

CHAPTER 12

Toby wiped snow off his watch and looked down at the compass pointer. 'It's that way,' he said. 'You go first, Abby, and then Andy can ski past you.'

Abby dug in her poles and slipped away through the soft new snow.

'Stop!' yelled Toby and Andy together.

She had gone only a few metres. She stopped, turned – and could see nothing at all! Everything was white. She felt panic wash over her, but then she heard Andy's voice.

'Come back,' he called. 'Over here.'

She looked down and saw the tracks of her skis. She almost laughed with relief, but then she thought of Hayley. They had to hurry. She moved as fast as she could towards Andy's voice, and after a few seconds the blurred shapes of the two boys appeared through the snow. Andy skied down to her.

'We'll have to be incredibly careful,' Abby told him. 'I thought I'd hardly moved, but when I turned round and couldn't see you, it was really scary. It's lucky the slope is so gentle.'

'Yell at me when you think I've gone far enough,' Andy said, and set off down the hill.

Almost at once, Abby called out, 'Stop!' Andy had all but vanished.

Toby joined her. 'We'll both go to Andy now,' he said. 'Then we can do the same thing again. It's not perfect, but at least we know we're going in roughly the right direction, and I can't think of a way of skiing and looking at a compass at the same time. As soon as the slope flattens out we'll know we're at the bottom of the hill. Then we can look for those trees.'

They carried on, taking it in turns to go ahead while Toby directed them. All the time, the snow swirled thickly around them. Abby didn't mind so much while she could see Andy's dim shape ahead of her, but when it was her turn to ski into the featureless whiteness, she felt dizzy and scared. It was only the slope of the hill that gave her any sense of which way she was facing. But she forced herself to stay calm. And now, as she skied off for the sixth or seventh time, there was no slope any more. She turned to call to the others, and for a moment she had no idea which way she was facing. Every direction was exactly the same. Then she saw a dark shape approaching and everything made sense again.

'This is great,' said Toby. 'We've made it to the bottom.'

'It doesn't *feel* great,' said Abby. 'It's really strange, but this feels just as scary as the blizzard in Austria a couple of years ago. Doesn't it, Andy?'

'It's bad,' he agreed.

'We won't go wrong,' Toby said. 'I checked before we set out. We go due west now. We can't help getting to those trees. They won't be more than a couple of hundred metres from here.'

'But what if we're not where we think we are?' asked Abby. She was very glad that Toby had come with them.

'Remember when we were on the moors back in October?' Toby said. 'And all that orien- teering? This is just the same.' He looked at his watch and set a bearing. 'That way.' He pointed. 'You go first, Andy. I reckon it'll take five minutes.'

As the snow drifted down thicker than ever, Abby found herself remembering that day on the moors: they'd had to find their way across in the mist and rain. She hadn't been scared then. It had been an exciting adventure. At least, it had been until she'd decided to climb down that cliff beside the waterfall and . . .

She glanced at Toby, standing beside her. He never seemed to be scared of anything, although she knew he'd sometimes been bullied at school. Priya had been scared on the moors, but she'd been brave too. She must have been terrified, but she'd got down that cliff even though she'd never climbed anything before. Neither had Jay—

'Abby,' prompted Toby. 'Andy's waiting. Don't worry. It seems really dangerous, but we know exactly what we're doing.'

It was strange, Abby thought as she looked gratefully at Toby and then moved off to join Andy – people at school thought Toby was just a geek. That was why he got picked on – because he'd rather spend his lunch breaks in the computer room than outside playing football. But those people didn't know him. His calm confidence was infectious: yes, they were doing all the right things—

'Abby!' called Andy. 'Stop! Where are you going?'

'Sorry,' she said as Andy and Toby joined her. 'I wasn't thinking.'

'Or you were thinking about something else,' said Toby. 'We have to concentrate all the time. We should see the trees any second. Let's go.'

Abby skied forward in the direction Toby was

pointing and suddenly an enormous shape loomed darkly through the snow. 'We're there,' she yelled excitedly. 'There's a tree!'

The others joined her quickly. They stood under branches that were bent down by the weight of newly fallen snow. The tree was a silver birch. The snow was less deep beneath the branches, and they could just make out the shapes of other trees nearby.

'Hayley!' called Abby. 'Can you hear me? Where are you?'

The others took up the cry, and for a minute or two they all shouted as loudly as they could, pausing occasionally to listen for a reply.

'She's not here,' Toby said at last. 'We should try and find that bench where Sean said he saw her. If we keep going south until the trees end, we'll be somewhere near it.'

'We should leave something here,' said Andy. 'A marker. It'll help us find our way back.'

'You're right,' said Toby. He pulled off his gloves with his teeth and took a knife from his pocket. He moved over to a nearby tree and cut a long section from the end of one of the branches, which he planted in the snow. Then he pulled something else from an inside pocket and fastened it to the top of the branch. 'That should do it.'

'Toby!' Abby couldn't help laughing. 'Why are you carrying a flag in your pocket?'

'I thought we might need it if we made a camp. Come on, let's move.'

The flag was soon lost to view as they worked their way from tree to tree. 'That's it. That was the last one,' Toby said after a few minutes.

He was interrupted by a shout from Andy. 'There's something over there,' he said. 'I think it's the bench.'

'It's not snowing so hard,' said Abby. 'If it had been, we'd never have seen it.'

'Someone's been here,' Toby said as they reached the bench. 'Look – even under all this new stuff you can see the snow was churned up.'

'And there's a snowman,' said Abby. 'You can

see where Hayley's been walking in the snow.'

They followed the indentations of Hayley's footprints until they reached the snowman. His head bristled with twigs. 'She must have collected them from the trees,' Abby muttered, 'before it started to snow. It's a spiky hairdo. She must be nearby. Let's call her again.'

'She must have gone somewhere else before it started to snow,' Toby said. 'Otherwise there'd be footprints.'

'I'm going to call her anyway.' Abby cupped her hands to her mouth and called, 'Hayley! Hayley, where are you?'

There was no reply. 'It's hardly snowing at all now,' said Andy. 'You can see the trees. Let's take our skis off and leave them here as a marker. Then we can spread out and search. She must be somewhere near here.'

'OK,' agreed Toby, and they made a pyramid of skis in the snow.

'Wait!' said Abby. 'What was that? Listen!'

They were all silent. Everything was very still.

Just a few flakes of snow were falling now. Then they heard it: a faint cry from somewhere ahead of them.

'Hayley?' yelled Abby. 'Is that you?'

They heard the voice again. 'It's straight ahead,' said Andy, pointing. 'Can you see anything? It feels like my eyes aren't working properly.'

Abby blinked. All she could see ahead of her was whiteness. There was nothing to tell her where the earth ended and the sky began. Then something moved. 'There!' she said. 'Hayley, is that you?'

There was a faint answering cry, and Abby saw another movement ahead of her. All at once she realized that she was looking at a small figure covered in snow. The figure moved again, and Abby's heart lurched. 'Don't worry,' she called. 'We're here now. We'll take you to your brother.'

They all started forward, but they had only taken two or three steps when they heard a different sound – one which made Abby's hair stand on end. A creaking noise came from beneath their feet.

'It's ice,' breathed Toby. 'We're standing on the lake. I'm going to move back. You two follow me, one at a time.'

'But what about Hayley?' cried Abby. 'We have to get her off there.'

'We can't all stand on here together,' said Toby urgently as he edged backwards. 'We can't stay on the ice at all. You heard it creaking. We have to get off it and then work out what to do. It won't help Hayley if the ice breaks.'

'Where are you going?' called Hayley in a trembling voice. 'I don't like it here. It went all snowy and I couldn't find anyone.'

'Just wait where you are,' called Toby as Abby and Andy both moved backwards.

'I can't tell if we're on the shore or not,' said Abby.

'We are now,' said Toby, scraping away at the snow with his boot. 'There isn't a proper bank here. The land just slopes really gently into the lake. That's why we walked straight onto the ice without noticing. It must be what Hayley did too.'

'But what are we going to do?' whispered Abby. 'I could go and get her. Maybe the ice only creaked because we were all standing together.'

'Bad idea,' said Andy, frowning. 'Hayley's only small. We can't tell how thick the ice is.'

'Or how thin,' Abby said, half to herself. 'We have to do *something*.'

'Remember what Rob told us?' Toby looked at the others. 'The first rule? Make sure *we're* safe.'

'Why are you all standing there?' demanded Hayley suddenly. 'Why are you whispering? I'm coming now.'

She had been kneeling on the ice. Suddenly she got to her feet and took a couple of steps towards them. The three Tigers watched, horrified, as her foot slipped and she went crashing to the ground. There was a loud thud, and then they all heard an ominous tearing, splitting sound that started near the little girl and seemed to shoot off into the distance.

'The ice is cracking,' said Toby. 'Stay there, Hayley! Whatever you do, don't move.'

'Why not?' Hayley cried. 'I want Lee. Why are you making me stay here? I won't.'

She climbed to her feet again, and instantly they heard the ice creak.

'Listen, Hayley,' said Abby, in the calmest voice she could manage. 'Where you're standing, it's on a big pond. You know, like the one in the park?'

As soon as the words were out of her mouth, Abby knew she'd said the wrong thing. She had a sudden vision of a gaping black hole in the ice where the police had told them Lee and Sean had fallen in, and she could see from the expression on Hayley's face that she was remembering the same thing.

'The ice won't break,' Abby called. 'Not if you stand still. Do you understand, Hayley? The ice only broke in the park because Lee and Sean were jumping around on it. They're much bigger than you. Just stay there and we'll get you off.'

'I want to get off now.' Hayley began to cry.

'I've got a rope,' said Toby, opening his pack and searching inside. 'I'm sure it's here somewhere.' He stopped and clapped his hand to his head. 'I don't believe it. It's in my other bag. It's back at the camp.'

'We'll have to try our skis,' suggested Andy. 'We could push one out to her.'

'They're not long enough,' said Abby. 'You know they're not.'

But Andy was already racing back through the snow to where they had left their skis.

'One of us can lie on the ice,' he said when he returned. 'I'll do it if you like. Then I can hold out the ski. It might just be long enough.'

'It's the right idea,' Toby said. 'Lying down spreads your weight out. And as long as we hold onto you it's safe enough.'

'And I'm the lightest,' said Abby, quickly lying down on the snow. 'You know I am. You two hold onto my feet.'

She grabbed the ski from Andy, then stretched

herself out and began to wriggle forwards, pushing the ski out in front of her. She could feel the two boys gripping her ankles, and that made her feel much safer. She moved very slowly, almost sure that she could feel the ice moving very slightly beneath her body. The tremor seemed to spread right through her, and she realized she was shivering violently.

'What is it?' asked Andy quietly. 'What's wrong?'

'I'm OK,' said Abby. She looked up at Hayley, just a few metres away, and forced herself to smile. 'Don't worry, Hayley. We're going to get you out of here.' She twisted round and saw that both boys were lying down, reaching out as far as they could.

'Stop there, Abby,' said Toby. 'Now push the ski as near to Hayley as you can.'

The little girl was trembling with fear. 'Can you get down on your knees?' Abby asked. 'Really gently. Then you can reach out for this ski. Look – I'm going to push it out to you.'

The ski inched forward over the surface as

Hayley knelt on the ice. She stretched out her hand, but Abby could already see that she was too far away.

'I can get it,' Hayley said. She leaned forward and put both her hands on the snow. Then she began to crawl towards Abby. As soon as she moved, there was a loud cracking sound.

'Stop!' yelled Abby, far louder than she had intended.

Hayley lifted her hands and there was another creak from the ice.

'Listen,' said Abby urgently. 'You mustn't move at all. Like when you're playing musical statues at a party – OK? You're going to have to be very brave. You're going to have to wait there while we find something long enough to reach you. You'll be all right as long as you don't move. Do you understand?'

Hayley nodded. Tears were rolling down her cheeks.

Abby looked back at the boys. 'Go and find something,' she said. 'There must be a fallen branch somewhere under those trees.'

'Good idea,' said Toby. 'Come on. We'll pull you back.'

'No,' said Abby. 'I can't leave Hayley. Not like this.'

'Sorry, Abby,' said Toby, pulling her back off the ice. 'You have to be on the shore . . . Abby's just moving back a little way,' he called to Hayley. 'But she's going to be right here until we're ready to rescue you. You're doing great.'

'Go on, then,' urged Abby. 'Be as quick as you can.'

· She paused. Toby was looking beyond her, at the flat apron of snow that covered the icy lake. He didn't say anything – just indicated with his head that she should look. Behind where Hayley knelt, a long narrow stain snaked across the snow. Water was seeping through the crack in the ice.

'Go!' whispered Abby. 'There's no time to waste.'

CHAPTER 13

Back in the temporary encampment, Connor glanced anxiously at his watch.

'How long have they been gone?' asked Jay, looking up from the almost-mended sledge.

'Nearly half an hour,' said Connor. 'I think the snow's easing up a bit. They're bound to find her soon.'

'I've got another screw ready, Jay,' said Hamish. 'Are you ready?'

'OK.' Jay grinned.

Hamish had watched, fascinated, as Jay searched all their sledges for screws that weren't completely essential and removed them to use in his repair. He had looked on in open-mouthed astonishment as Jay opened the saw tool on Connor's precious Swiss Army knife, removed a section of wood from the top of the sledge, then used another tool to make holes in the wood. He had appointed himself Jay's assistant, and had forgotten all about his injured leg and Lee and his friends, who were huddled together in a corner of the shelter under the watchful eyes of Mrs Johnston and Mrs Mitchell.

Priya was still telling stories to the other children. Connor was astonished at how many she knew. Now she had started one about a cat and a parrot, and he found himself listening, in spite of his worry about the other Tigers and the little girl.

'Slip, slop,' said Priya, in a very cat-like voice. 'Down the cat's throat went the parrot!'

All the children laughed, but suddenly Lee was on his feet, shouting. 'You're all just sitting here like this is some kind of a party. My sister's out there lost in the snow and you aren't doing a thing.'

Connor turned on him. 'My friends are looking for her,' he said hotly. 'Someone has to look after all these other children, and Abby and Andy and Toby have got proper clothes and equipment. They know what they're doing.'

'Connor is right,' Mrs Johnston told Lee. 'It would be madness for all of us to go stumbling around in this weather. When those three find your sister, they'll call me, and then we can decide what to do next. Just calm down. I'll call the police again and see if there's any news.'

She made the call, but all the police vehicles were still immobilized by the storm. 'They say they hope the worst will be over in the next hour or so,' she said. 'The Search and Rescue team are making their way out here on foot, but it's going to take them some time.'

'They're rubbish,' said Lee. 'Look – it's hardly snowing at all now. Here, have your stupid jacket back.' He pulled Connor's spare waterproof off and flung it on the ground. 'I've got to go and find her. Get out of my way.'

Mrs Johnston took hold of his arm, but he

pushed her aside roughly and stumbled out of the shelter.

'Stop!' yelled Connor. 'You'll get lost.'

Lee ignored him. He kept on walking, heading downhill. Connor followed him out of the shelter. There was a sudden flurry of heavy snow, and a squall whipped it into his face. He wiped it away, and when he looked again, Lee had gone.

Connor turned round and saw everyone watching him. 'I shouldn't have shouted at him,' he said. He still felt angry, but now he was angry with himself. His temper had caused trouble before. He glanced at Jay.

'He would have gone anyway,' Jay told him, almost as if he was reading his mind. He looked up from the lashing he was putting around the newly-mended sledge rail. 'You couldn't have stopped him.'

'Jay's right,' said Mrs Johnston. 'But maybe one of us grown-ups should go after him.'

Connor shook his head. 'It's pointless,' he said.

'He could be absolutely anywhere. We'll just have to wait for the snow to stop. And hope that he's all right.'

Lee's three friends had said nothing at all during all this, but now Sean spoke: 'He never wanted to bring Hayley in the first place. His mum said he had to.'

'I thought she'd be all right, messing around making that snowman,' said one of the others. 'She will be OK, won't she?'

Connor opened his mouth to speak, but then shook his head and looked away, disgusted. He looked at his watch anxiously. 'They must have found something by now,' he said. 'Why don't they call? Mrs Johnston, can't you call Toby and find out what's happening?'

'Of course,' she said. 'I'll do it now.'

Abby lay shivering as the snow came down thickly again and the wind howled. It was horrible, being able to see Hayley's terrified eyes just a few metres away and not being able to cuddle her. Abby remembered suddenly how Andy had kept talking to her when she'd got stuck on the cliff, and she knew that she had to take Hayley's mind off things. 'I liked your snowman,' she said. 'Why did you give him that hairdo?'

'I . . . I wanted to make him like Jason Gold,' Hayley said. 'I like him. He's on *The X Factor*.'

'He could be a singing snowman,' suggested Abby. The snow was so thick again now that she could hardly make out Hayley's face. 'Hey, listen – we could sing "Frosty the Snowman". Do you know it?' She started to sing.

Hayley managed a half-smile, and began to join in very quietly.

As Abby sang her way through the song, the little girl began to cheer up. Before the end, Abby came to a stop. 'I don't know what comes next,' she said.

'I do,' replied Hayley. 'It's when we stamp around the classroom.' And at that point she brought her hand down with a thump on the snow. At once there was another cracking sound, and Abby's heart leaped into her mouth. Both girls were very still for a moment, but nothing else happened.

'It's OK,' said Abby, keeping her voice very calm, although her heart was thudding so hard she thought it might crack the ice all by itself. 'You didn't do any harm. But maybe we should try a quieter song.'

She began to sing. '*Hush little baby, don't say a word—*'

'Abby, look!' said Hayley.

Abby turned and saw the boys coming towards them, dragging something behind them. 'What is it?' she called.

'We found a branch,' Andy said. 'It was buried under piles of snow.'

'Be quick,' Abby whispered. 'Hayley's terrified.'

'Who wouldn't be?' said Toby.

'It's not a very thick branch.' Abby looked at the slender piece of wood that ended in ice-covered twigs. 'Are you sure it's going to be strong enough?'

'It'll have to be,' said Andy grimly. 'Let's give it a try.'

'OK, Hayley,' said Abby. 'We're going to push the branch out to you really carefully. Wait until it's really close to you before you try to grab it.'

'All right.' Hayley's voice sounded very small. Large flakes of snow were still falling around them.

The two boys took the thick end of the branch and manoeuvred it into place on the edge of the ice.

'Really slowly,' said Toby, and Abby watched the twiggy end creep closer and closer to where Hayley was kneeling.

'Wait!' shouted Abby. 'Hayley ought to lie down on the ice. You can do that, can't you?' she said to Hayley. 'Just like I did. It won't be for long.'

But Abby was too late. Hayley had seen that the end of the branch was almost within reach and she pushed herself upright and stretched out her hand. She took a small step forward and grabbed. There was a loud snap, and a long piece of the branch broke off.

Hayley fell forward heavily, and there was a horrible splitting sound from the ice – a creaking and a cracking and a tearing that seemed to spread all over the flat expanse of snow that concealed the deep water beneath.

'Be quick,' urged Abby. 'Push it out to her. What are you waiting for?'

The boys were staring at the lake in horror. Further out, the water was bubbling up through the ice, darkening the snow. Suddenly Toby's phone began to ring in his pocket, but he ignored it.

'Come on,' repeated Abby urgently. 'You have to do it now.'

Andy moved first. He picked up the branch and pushed it forward. Abby took hold of one end and wriggled onto the ice, feeling Toby grab hold of her ankles. She shoved the branch towards Hayley, who was now lying down on her stomach, sobbing and shaking.

'You can do it,' said Abby. 'Try to get hold of a thick bit. Do it as gently as you can.'

Hayley took hold of a piece of the branch and looked fearfully at Abby.

'That's it. Now hold tight. We're going to pull you in like a sledge. OK . . . *pull.*'

Hayley began to move slowly over the surface, clinging on to the thin piece of wood. Seconds later she was close enough for Abby to reach out and pull her onto the shore. She lifted the little girl up and hugged her tightly as she sobbed. She hardly noticed the tears that were streaming down her own cheeks.

Andy picked up the branch and stamped on it. It snapped into three pieces. 'It was rotten,' he said. 'It's lucky it didn't break before.'

He picked up the longest bit and flung it out through the falling snow onto the lake. There was a crunch, and a dark hole appeared in the snow. Water spread quickly over the surface.

From all over the lake Abby could hear the sound of the ice coming apart.

Another minute, she thought. *Another minute and we would have been too late.*

CHAPTER 14

Abby hugged Hayley tighter and felt her shivering. 'She's cold,' she said to Toby. 'And so am I.'

They walked as quickly as they could back to where they had left the skis. 'Right,' said Toby, taking off his rucksack and pulling out his flask. 'It's lucky I brought this. Do you like hot chocolate, Hayley?'

He poured some steaming liquid into the top of the flask as Hayley looked up and nodded. Abby started to put her down, but Hayley clung on even more tightly, and Toby handed her the cup. Abby helped her to take small sips as Toby took out his phone and called Mrs Johnston.

'We've found her,' he said. 'She's safe. She's just having a hot drink, then we're going to start back.'

Toby listened for a moment, then looked at Hayley and moved away from the others, talking urgently into the phone. Abby knew that he was worried about hypothermia. Hayley was only small and she'd been out in the cold for a long time. She was still shivering and looked very pale, even though they'd wrapped all their spare clothing around her.

Toby rang off. Abby stared at the deep snow all around them. 'We'll have to carry her,' she said to Toby. 'We can take it in turns. Here, Andy. You carry my skis.'

Andy and Toby fastened the skis to their backpacks, and Abby lifted Hayley onto her back. 'Hey!' she said as Hayley wrapped her arms tightly around her neck. 'There's no need to strangle me.'

Hayley didn't reply, but she relaxed her grip the tiniest bit.

'All right,' said Toby. 'We can follow our tracks back to the marker. It should be easy. Look for the trail our branch made.'

The snow kept on falling as they made their way back to the trees. 'That's where we found it,' said Toby, pointing to an area of disturbed snow.

'It was incredibly lucky,' said Abby, trying to ignore the pain in her back from carrying Hayley.

'Not really,' replied Andy. 'Toby thought everything out. We didn't waste time looking anywhere else, just under the trees. This was the fourth one we tried.'

'Anyone would have thought of it,' said Toby.

'No they wouldn't,' Abby insisted. 'That's why you're Assistant Patrol Leader.'

'Come on,' replied Toby gruffly. 'We follow the trees to the marker.'

'Hey, Hayley,' said Andy. 'Come and ride on me for a while. Abby needs a rest.'

Hayley's arms gripped Abby's neck even tighter.

'Abby's getting tired,' he went on firmly. 'Let me carry you for a little while.'

Hayley reluctantly allowed Andy to take her, and Abby sighed with relief as they followed after

Toby. 'Isn't this snow ever going to stop?' she said as the flakes continued to swirl around them. 'I'm fed up with not being able to see anything.'

'I can see something,' Andy said. 'Toby's found the flag. We'll soon be back,' he told Hayley. 'You'll see your brother again.'

'I feel sleepy,' murmured Hayley.

'Don't go to sleep, Hayley.' Abby felt anxiety tugging at her stomach. 'Keep talking to me.'

They found Toby taking a careful bearing. 'You can still see our tracks . . . just,' he said. 'We go east along the foot of the hill. The tricky bit will be finding where to start climbing.'

'We should have left a marker there too,' said Andy.

'I know,' replied Toby, nodding. 'Another time, that's what I'll do.'

'We have to hurry,' Abby said quietly to Toby. 'Hayley's sleepy and she's still cold. Is there help coming?'

'Soon,' said Toby briefly. 'It's my turn to carry Hayley, Andy. Pass her over.'

Hayley livened up a little as Toby took her. 'You're not very big,' she said. 'Are you sure you're strong enough?'

'Of course I am,' said Toby, handing his rucksack and skis to Abby and hoisting Hayley onto his back.

'Hey, wait a minute,' said Abby when she felt the weight of the rucksack. 'This thing is heavier than Hayley. I'm sure it is.'

Toby laughed. 'You see,' he told Hayley. 'Carrying my heavy rucksack around has made me strong. Let's go. The hill is up there to our left, remember. We need to keep as close as we can to where the land starts going uphill.'

'Shouldn't we count our steps?' asked Abby. 'We couldn't when we were on skis.'

'It won't matter, will it?' said Andy. 'We'll hear them blowing the whistle.'

'I don't know how far the sound will carry in the snow,' said Toby. 'Abby's right. I know we're in a hurry, but it's best to be careful. It worked on the Search and Rescue exercise, didn't it? And this kind of thing is exactly what we were practising for. I normally do eighty double paces to a hundred metres and we should add ten per cent for the deep snow, so that's eighty-eight. We should all do it. Even if we don't start up the hill at exactly the right place, it should get us close enough to hear them. If we haven't heard anything after five minutes, we should stop and rethink.'

They repeated the procedure they'd followed earlier. Abby set off into the blinding whiteness. The faint outline of their tracks made it slightly easier, and she concentrated on counting her steps. She stopped when Andy shouted. He came past her, and she let his outline almost fade away before she called to him. They seemed to Abby to be moving forward unbearably slowly.

Toby moved up to join her. 'I'm going to stay at the back with Hayley,' he said. 'I'll keep checking your direction. Are you all right, Hayley?'

'I'd like to go to bed,' Hayley murmured. 'Where's my teddy?'

Toby glanced at Abby. Hayley was disorientated, and they both knew that this was a symptom of hypothermia. 'Go on,' he said. 'As quickly as you can.'

Abby caught up with Andy. 'Keep listening,' she said. 'As soon as we hear Connor's whistle we can head towards it. There's no time to lose.'

She floundered on through the deep snow. When she found herself climbing slightly, she remembered Toby's words and altered course.

'That's far enough,' called Andy. He followed in her tracks and overtook her.

Toby rejoined her. 'I don't think it's snowing quite so hard,' Abby told him. 'Andy's gone a lot further than before and I can still see him.'

'Good,' said Toby. 'But don't let him go too far. What if it gets thicker again? Hey, Andy! Stop!'

Abby tramped forward, almost running. 'We have to move faster,' she said as she passed Andy. Moments later her foot sank unexpectedly deeply into the snow and she only just managed to keep her feet. She plunged on quickly, hoping Andy hadn't seen, counting under her breath – eighty-six, eighty-seven, eighty-eight, eighty-nine, ninety, ninety-one. She stopped. 'That's it!' she yelled. 'A hundred metres.'

She turned – and saw nothing but whiteness. Just for a moment she panicked, but then she looked down and saw the clear line of footprints in the snow – and there were Andy and Toby, materializing slowly out of the falling snow as they walked towards her.

Andy was shaking his head as he came up to her. 'You're never going to change, are you?' he said.

'I didn't mean . . . I was just trying to get us back quickly . . . I'm sorry.'

'It's OK,' said Toby. 'We know. I think we should start going uphill now.'

Hayley stirred in Toby's arms and opened her eyes. 'Are we nearly there?' she asked.

Abby laughed in spite of her anxiety. 'I suppose you say that all the time when you go out in the car?'

But Hayley had closed her eyes again. Abby could hear that her breathing was shallow and uneven.

Toby hugged her closer, trying to warm her. 'Go, Andy,' he said, looking at the compass in his watch and holding out one arm. 'Straight up there.'

They struggled up the hill. Abby could see that Toby was finding it very hard work with Hayley in his arms, and she was about to shout to him that it was *her* turn to carry her again when she saw an indistinct shape away to her right.

'Andy, stop!' she yelled. 'Come back here. I think I saw something.'

Toby put on a spurt and joined them, gasping for breath. 'What was it? What did you see? It can't be the camp because we would have heard a whistle.'

'It was over there,' Abby said.

'I can't see a thing.'

'Are you sure—?' began Andy. But suddenly

the shape was there again. Something was moving.

'Hey!' yelled Abby. 'Who's that? Can you hear me?'

The shape seemed to come nearer for a few moments, then it veered off into the snow again.

'What is it?' said Hayley, woken by the shouting and looking around wildly. 'It's not a wolf, is it?'

'There aren't any wolves,' Abby reassured her. 'Everyone yell. Come on.'

They all called out as loudly as they could, and the shape stopped moving.

'I'll go and see who it is,' Abby said, and before the others could stop her, she was off. Immediately the dark shape solidified into a person. Whoever it was stood very still. A few metres further and she recognized Lee. He was shaking with the cold, and hardly seemed to recognize Abby.

'Come with me,' she said, reaching out and

taking hold of his arm. 'We're just over there. We've found your sister.'

Lee stared at her. 'What?'

'We've found Hayley. Come on. You're freezing. We have to get back to the others.'

She tugged at Lee's arm, and he began to walk, hardly able to lift his feet far enough out of the snow to take each step.

'It's Lee,' Abby called as they neared the others. 'Come here, quickly!'

'Lee?' said Hayley, stirring in Toby's arms. 'Lee?'

Lee looked down at her. 'I was looking for you,' he said. 'Honest, I was. I never meant to leave you on your own. It started snowing and we couldn't find you. Are you OK? Hayley? Talk to me.'

Hayley closed her eyes. 'What's wrong with her?' Lee demanded wildly. 'Give her to me. What have you done to her?'

'Quiet!' ordered Toby. 'Listen!'

Faintly through the falling snow came the sound of six blasts on a whistle.

'It's them,' Toby said. 'We're almost there.' He took out his own whistle and blew three short blasts.

'You're mental,' yelled Lee. 'Blowing whistles! Give her to me.' He made a grab for Hayley and fell full-length in the snow.

'I've got him,' said Abby, pulling Lee to his feet. He pushed her away, but she took his arm firmly and felt him trembling. 'The whistle is the International Distress Signal,' she told him. 'It's going to get you and your sister back to safety, OK? Six blasts followed by a one-minute gap. Listen – there it is again. And the reply is three blasts.'

Lee didn't reply. He was exhausted and trembling, and he kept stumbling as they walked forward together through the snow.

'I can see the shelter,' called Andy. 'We're there!'

Then Abby saw the tall, unmistakable shape of Connor standing beside the wall of snow. Seconds later she was surrounded by Priya and Jay and Connor, and all the little children.

'Brilliant, you guys!' said Connor. 'I knew you'd do it.'

Then he saw the look on Abby's face – suddenly she was close to tears. 'We have to get Hayley to hospital,' she said. 'We have to do it fast.'

And as she said it, Lee's legs gave way beneath him, and he sank to the ground.

CHAPTER 15

'Get him into the shelter, quickly,' said Connor urgently. 'Everyone find all the spare clothes you've got. I'll get a foil blanket. Mrs Johnston, can you find out what's happening with the police?'

The whole shelter became a flurry of activity. Priya lit Toby's stove and started heating water for drinks. Lee was quickly wrapped in warm clothes and then enfolded in the blanket.

'I've got the Search and Rescue team on the phone,' Mrs Johnston told Connor. 'They want to talk to you.'

'Hi, Connor.' It was Rob. His voice sounded loud in Connor's ear. 'We need information about your casualties.'

'Where are you?' asked Connor. 'I think the

little girl ought to get to hospital as soon as possible. She was out on the ice and she was on her own in the snow for quite a long time.'

'Hold on,' said Rob. 'Slow down, Connor. Tell me about the little girl's condition. Do you think she's cold? How's her breathing.'

Connor took a deep breath. 'She's very pale and she's shivering. Her breathing is a bit shallow. We've given her hot drinks and she's wrapped up well, but she's very groggy and I don't think she really knows where she is.'

'OK,' said Rob. 'You've done well, Connor. The snow's eased off and there won't be much more. I'm going to call in a helicopter now. Give me a couple of minutes and I'll ring you back on this phone. Do you think you'll be able to get your casualties off the hill and down to the flat area near the car park?'

'Well, yes . . .' began Connor.

'Then you should get ready to move,' Rob told him. 'I'll call you in a moment.'

'We have to pack everything up,' Connor said

to the Tigers. 'Is the sledge you mended OK, Jay?'

'I'm just about to check,' he replied. 'Come on, Hamish – you can sit on it if you like. Be careful of your knee.'

'Cool,' said Hamish, sitting on the sledge. 'Pull me as fast as you can.'

'You're a casualty,' Jay said. 'I'll give you a nice smooth ride.'

'Be quick,' Connor told him.

'It's as good as new,' Jay reported, after pulling the loaded sledge along for a little way.

'Great. We're going to need it,' said Connor. 'We have to get everyone down to the car park as soon as we can.'

Snow was still drifting down, but it was falling less thickly now. A heavy shower had just passed and Connor could see another one approaching from the west. In the gap between the heavy grey clouds, a sudden flash of blue sky appeared.

The Tigers were all busy. Priya and Andy were taking down the wall of sledges and helping the children to gather up their things. The phone rang in Connor's hand. 'We're nearly ready to move,' he told Rob. 'What do you want us to do?'

'The helicopter will land due west of the car park,' Rob said. 'Get everyone down the hill and into the car park itself, OK? The helicopter won't land until the crew can see that you're all there. Is that understood?'

'I've got it,' replied Connor. 'All of us into the car park before the helicopter lands.'

'Good,' said Rob. 'Now I need to know about your other casualties. The little boy first.'

Connor explained about the cut in Hamish's knee and the big splinter of wood embedded in it. He described what Toby had done.

'Exactly right,' said Rob. 'It doesn't sound too serious, but you can't be too careful with things like that. And you say there's another boy.'

'His name's Lee,' Connor said. 'I think he's about fourteen, a bit taller than me but not really very fit. He's been out in the snow for quite a long time.'

'Well, you know the drill. Give him a hot

drink and some high-energy food if you have some. Keep him warm. Continue to check on the casualties and note any changes in their condition. The helicopter will be there in ten minutes, and we should get there at about the same time. Good luck. Oh, and Connor, you've all done a great job out there. Brilliant, mate!'

Connor felt very proud of the Tigers. Rob was right – they'd done really well, all of them. The gear was all packed now, and stowed neatly on the sledges, and the Scouts were ready to load up their passengers.

'Here you are, Hayley,' Abby said as Mrs Johnston looked on anxiously. 'We've made you a bed on this sledge.'

She laid Hayley gently on the sledge, all bundled up in every piece of spare clothing they'd been able to find, and then wrapped in a space-blanket and a plastic sheet. Only her nose and eyes were visible. Abby put two straps around her to stop her falling off, then looked up at Connor. 'We should get moving,' she said.

Connor nodded agreement, and turned to where Lee was sitting with his friends.

'We'd better put him on the big sledge,' Toby said quietly. 'We'll have to do this on foot. I'm not sure I can pull the weight with skis on.'

'That's fine,' said Connor. 'Mrs Johnston and Mrs Mitchell don't have skis anyway, and we should all keep together. I'll tell Lee.'

He went over to where the boys were sitting. Lee was shivering uncontrollably, despite the extra clothes he was wearing and the blanket wrapped around him. 'You'll need to lie on my big sledge,' Connor told him. 'It'll be safer. There's a helicopter coming to take your sister to hospital. And you too, probably.'

'I'm OK,' said Lee, with a flash of his usual surliness. 'I can walk.'

'We haven't got time for this.' Connor's voice was calm, but there was a edge to it. 'You're tired and you're ill. You'll slow us down, and there are other people here who need treatment more urgently than you do.'

'You can't tell me what to do.' Lee took off the foil blanket and got unsteadily to his feet. A surprised look passed over his face. He staggered and fell heavily against Sean, who had to hold him upright.

'Honest, Lee,' said Sean. 'You'd better go on the sledge.'

'Just wait a bit. I'll be OK.'

'No you won't,' said Sean, and Connor heard the anger in his voice. 'This whole thing was your stupid idea, and it's your fault our sledge is lost out there somewhere. I don't know why we ever listened to you.'

Lee's face turned ugly. He put up a hand and tried to push it into Sean's face, but Sean simply grabbed his arm and pulled it down again. He gave Lee a shove and Lee fell backwards onto Toby's sledge. He tried to sit up again, but Connor could see that there was something funny about his eyes.

'Toby, Andy, Abby,' he said. 'Help me, quick. We have to lift him over onto my sledge. One on each corner. One . . . two . . . three . . . lift. OK. Now put that blanket and plastic sheet over him, Toby, and then these straps.'

Lee's face was even paler than before. Connor bent close to his face. He was breathing, but he didn't sound good. Connor checked the pulse in his neck. It was weak and irregular.

'Let's move,' he said. 'We'll go to our left, across the slope of the hill. That way the sledges won't run away with us. Will you be OK, Mrs Johnston? Mrs Mitchell?'

'We have much worse snow than this in the Highlands,' said Mrs Mitchell. 'We're used to it. Off you go.'

The Scouts set off in convoy, with Toby in the lead, pulling Hayley on his sledge. Jay was pulling Hamish on the one he had mended.

'It's a good job you didn't cut the rope,' Mrs Johnston said to Connor. 'And as for your sledge-mending skills, young man' – she turned to Jay – 'well, I think Hamish is going to be your friend for life!'

A little while later they had all reached the flat ground at the foot of the hill. The snow had almost stopped now, and Connor watched as Toby headed out across the open ground towards the car park, then stopped for a moment, looking at something away to his right.

'It's the lake,' said Andy, turning back to Connor, and Connor saw that his face was pale. When he looked at the lake, he saw why. It was no longer a sheet of clean white snow. There was a black hole quite near the edge where dark water rippled. As they watched, a couple of ducks flew overhead and landed on the water in a chorus of harsh quacking. Dark lines snaked all over the surface where water had been seeping up through the cracks in the ice and melting the snow.

'We were quite safe, you know,' Andy told Connor. 'We were very careful.'

'We have to hurry,' Connor said, bending to check Lee's breathing and pulse again. It was the same as before. Ahead of him he saw Toby checking on Hayley. He gave Connor a thumbs-up and then moved off towards the car park. The little girl was alive, but if the ice had given way a moment sooner . . . Connor knew it would be a long time before he could get the sight of that gaping black hole in the ice out of his mind.

As he watched the line of sledges strung out in front of him, Connor thought of his grandpa's stories of expeditions in Norway. Maybe they had been a bit like this. Suddenly the sun broke through the ragged black clouds, sending long shadows leaping across the snow. From some-where above and ahead of them Connor heard the distant throb of an engine. 'As fast as you can!' he called. 'Everyone into the car park.'

He put on a final spurt. The big sledge, with Lee's weight on it, was feeling heavier with every step he took. As he entered the car park, he stumbled and fell, and felt strong arms lifting him to his feet again. 'Rob!' he said, looking up at the bearded face. 'You made it.'

'Good lad,' said Rob, kneeling beside the sledge and checking Lee's condition.

There was a sudden loud clattering roar over-head, and Connor looked up to see the orange helicopter hovering above them.

'Not a moment too soon,' said Rob, standing up. 'Connor, you look dead on your feet. Sit down over here, mate. You've done your job. We'll take it from here.' He took a large flask out of his rucksack and handed it to him. 'Drink,' he said. 'Pass it round to your friends.'

Connor sat down on a bench that Toby had cleared of snow, and felt relief and tiredness wash over him as he swallowed the hot blackcurrant drink. Evie was checking Hayley, Abby looking on anxiously beside her, and Soraya was exam-ining Hamish's knee.

Andy sat down beside Connor, fumbling urgently with the fastenings of his rucksack. 'I have to get my camcorder,' he said. 'My fingers aren't working properly.'

The huge helicopter was turning round in the air. Andy tugged his camera bag out and began to film as it descended slowly towards the ground, sending a new blizzard of snow in every direction. Then it was down, and two paramedics and a doctor were running towards them. Rob directed the doctor to Hayley first, and Connor saw that she was asking Abby a string of questions. Then Hayley was transferred to a stretcher and carried over to the helicopter.

'Toby, Connor, could you give Doctor Wilson some information about Lee and Hamish?'

The doctor knelt down beside Lee, feeling for the pulse at his neck. Connor thought she looked very young. 'It was very faint when I first checked, fifteen minutes ago,' he told her, checking his watch. 'His breathing's been like that all the time since he collapsed. Before that he was wandering around in the snow for at least forty-five minutes. That's his sister over there.'

'Hamish cut his knee about two hours ago,' Toby said. 'We've been keeping an eye on him, but his temperature is OK and he seems fine apart from the lump of wood in his leg. In fact, it's hard to get him to stop talking.'

The two paramedics joined the doctor and transferred Lee to a stretcher. 'I think he'll be OK,' Dr Wilson told them. 'Thanks to you. I wouldn't have given much for his chances if you hadn't got some warm clothes on him. As for Hamish, I think we'll take him to hospital too. You were right – it's much the safest place to remove that piece of wood.'

Dr Wilson followed the stretchers to the helicopter and Rob came over to join the Scouts. 'Mrs Johnston, there's room for you to go in the helicopter with Hamish,' he said. 'The rest of you – we managed to get our vehicles halfway up the hill out of town. If you can make it down there, we'll give you a ride home.'

'I'm never going to get a ride in a helicopter, am I?' said Andy. 'Oh well, at least I can film it taking off. It's going to make a great movie.'

'If I come with you,' Mrs Johnston asked Rob, 'would you be able to take me to the hospital?'

'Sure,' agreed Rob. 'No problem.'

'Well, then,' said Mrs Johnston. 'You go in my

place, Andy. You helped to rescue that little girl, and I'm sure Hamish will give you some advice about your movie. Besides, he'll enjoy the footage of him in the helicopter.'

'You mean it?' Andy stood up, hastily gathering his things together. 'I can really go? What about the others?'

'It's the perfect end to your movie,' said Connor. 'Search and Rescue in action! It has to be you. We don't mind, do we?'

A paramedic was beckoning. 'Go on,' laughed Mrs Johnston. 'We'll look after your stuff. You've earned it!'

Andy grabbed his camcorder and ran across to the door of the helicopter.

CHAPTER 16

For a moment Hamish's grinning face filled the big screen in the Conference Centre at the country park, then the camera panned round to show the paramedics tending to Lee and Hayley. 'That was me,' came Hamish's voice from the back of the room. 'But I wasn't really ill.'

Abby heard laughter ripple around the audience. It was the Winter Sports Day, and every Scout Troop in Matfield was here, along with their parents and friends. Rick and Julie had agreed that it was the perfect occasion for the Tigers to persuade people to volunteer for the Search and Rescue team. Abby knew that Andy had been working day and night to get his movie ready in time, and it had been worth all the effort.

Up on the screen, the camera was pointing out

of the window of the helicopter, giving a bird's-eye view of the snowy landscape. Now there were houses with their roofs covered in snow, and roads blocked with abandoned cars, and suddenly there was the hospital, and the helipad, with its giant H coming closer and closer. The camera spun round towards the cockpit as the helicopter touched down, then pointed out of the open door to show the figures running across the helipad with stretchers. Finally it cut to a shot of a laughing Hamish, his knee neatly bandaged, leaving the hospital with his mum.

The titles appeared over shots of Matfield in the snow.

A FILM BY ANDY MACKENZIE
THANKS TO:
TIGER PATROL
SIXTH MATFIELD SCOUT TROOP
MATFIELD ASSOCIATION OF LOWLAND SEARCH
AND RESCUE
MATFIELD HELICOPTER AMBULANCE

The room filled with loud applause. Abby squeezed Andy's arm beside her. 'Come on,' she said. 'You have to take a bow, and then we must give our talk.'

Andy got to his feet reluctantly and went to the front of the room, where Rick and Julie were standing, beckoning to him. 'Our film-maker,' Rick told the audience. 'Andy Mackenzie.'

There was more cheering, then Rick held up a hand for silence. 'Those of you who know our Troop will be aware that Tiger Patrol have acquired the nickname Survival Squad. They certainly seem to have lived up to that on this occasion. But they haven't asked you here just to show you a movie. I know there's something else they want to tell you about.'

Connor stepped forward in front of the other Tigers. He cleared his throat nervously and glanced at the front row, where the entire Sutcliff family was sitting and smiling encouragement.

'We'd like to give you a short presentation about the work of the Lowland Search and

Rescue team,' Connor began as Jay and Toby bent over a laptop and a photo of the team appeared on the screen. 'As you can see, there aren't many of them, and they'd really like to recruit more volunteers. Here's what they do.'

Connor's voice grew in confidence as he explained the information that appeared on the screen. The other Tigers each presented a short section, and then it was Abby's turn.

'The team are often called out to help to organize searches if people go missing,' she told the audience. 'And sometimes . . .' She found herself suddenly struggling over her words as an image of Hayley, alone on the ice, came into her mind. She took a deep breath and finished her speech: 'Sometimes they have to search for missing children. It's really important work, and it would be great if you could help.'

Connor took over again as Abby sat down. 'Well done,' whispered Andy.

The final slide showed Rob walking beside a stretcher towards the helicopter. 'The Search and

Rescue team helped the police and the ambulance service to co-ordinate this operation,' Connor said. 'If you think you could help them, then Rob and Evie are waiting over there to take your names. Please think about joining up.'

'Thanks, Connor,' said Rick as enthusiastic applause rang around the room. 'And now, everyone, we're almost ready to begin our Winter Olympics. As you know, there will be gold, silver and bronze medals for each event, but we wanted to add something a little extra. Many of our Scouts haven't tried any snowsports before, so we've invited along some instructors from the Snow World dry ski slope. Everyone who tries an activity can earn points for their team – and for those of you who've been using this cold weather to try for your Snowsports Badges, the instructors will be able to do an assessment. Oh, and there's a barbecue in the car park. Now, the first event is the skating. We've got relay races coming up, and Toby here will explain how they're organized.'

Outside the Conference Centre, the Tigers

gathered together to prepare for the skating.

'Did you see all those people talking to Rob?' Jay said. 'It's really worked. It's a shame we're not old enough – we could all join up.'

'It was Andy's film that did it,' Abby said. 'It was completely amazing.'

Andy blushed. 'We're supposed to be getting ready,' he mumbled. 'Priya should definitely skate last, but who's going to go first?'

'Me, of course,' said Abby. 'Don't worry,' she told them, seeing the surprise on their faces. 'I came out here with Priya during the week. I've been practising.'

'She's pretty good,' said Priya. 'Very fast . . . as long as she doesn't fall over.'

'Hey! You know I don't—' Abby looked up from lacing her skates and saw they were all laughing.

'Serves you right,' said Andy. 'You're not the only one who knows how to wind people up! Come on – they're calling us. Let's show them how it's done!'

'And don't forget, we're not the Tigers today,' added Connor, quickly handing out a set of red, white and blue flags for them to pin to their clothes. *'Nous sommes la France!'*

Each Troop had been assigned a country chosen at random by Toby and Jay, who had spent at least as long planning the day's timetable as Andy had making his movie. They made their way to the edge of the ice, where the teams of Norway, Canada and the USA had gathered for the first heat. A large crowd had assembled on the terraced area outside the Conference Centre. Abby saw Andy's mum and dad, and Jay's – and there was Toby's mum looking really cool, her hair beautifully braided into intricate patterns. She waved at Abby and pointed beside her, where Abby's mum was standing – but it wasn't her mum Abby was looking for. Her dad had promised he'd be there, but she couldn't see him anywhere.

Pete walked over to join them, still limping slightly. 'I'm the starter and the referee,' he told them. 'Make sure you go round the *outside* of all the cones – there are judges out there watching. Start on my whistle, and touch hands to change over to the next skater.'

Abby took up her position, glancing to either side of her, trying to assess how confident the other skaters were. The tall boy next to her had the look of an athlete, but he didn't seem that steady on his skates.

'Ready!' called Pete, and then his whistle blew and Abby was away.

After a few short strides to get herself moving, she settled into a steady rhythm. She crouched low, trying to force real power into her movements as she pushed off from one skate onto the other. At first she didn't try to see where the other skaters were, but as she neared the far end of the ice she risked a look. The two skaters from Norway and Canada were nowhere, but the tall boy with the Stars and Stripes fluttering on his trousers was keeping up with her. His technique was rubbish, Abby decided, but he made up for it with sheer strength.

The turn was approaching fast, and Abby felt a moment of tension as she switched to the crossover step she'd learned from Priya, putting her weight onto the outside edge of her left skate and bringing the inside edge of her right round in front. It felt great. She had to trust the edge as she shifted her weight – it reminded her of the short radius turns on skis.

She completed the turn, and as she moved off smoothly back down the straight she heard a yell behind her. She glanced back and saw the tall boy climbing painfully back to his feet. When she handed over to Jay, she had a lead of forty metres, and as Jay skated away, the others surrounded her, patting her on the back. Then she saw the tall boy walking off the ice, and broke away to speak to him. 'Bad luck,' she said sympathetically. 'Are you OK?'

He grimaced. 'I'm not really a skater,' he said. 'Last week was the first time I tried. I don't think I'll do it again. It looks like your team are going to win.'

Andy was skating now and he was miles ahead. '*Allez, la France!*' yelled Andy's dad from the terrace.

The tall boy laughed. 'I'm Tom Glazer,' he said, offering his hand to Abby. 'Maybe I'll see you around.'

Tom went off to join his Troop, and Abby turned back to the ice just in time to see Priya coming in very comfortably in first place.

'Cool,' said Connor. 'We're in the final.'

As he sat and watched the other races, Connor realized that the final was going to be a lot tougher than the heat. Two of the winning teams had several skaters who looked very experienced, and Connor knew that, of the Tigers, only Priya could match them. When the final began, Abby skated first again, but this time she struggled to keep up with the other skaters, and by the time it was Connor's turn, France were last by a good ten metres, and the leading team – the Russians – were thirty metres in front of him.

He skated as fast as he knew how, and his ankles and legs were on fire as he battled down the home straight, but he knew that the others were drawing away from him. The Tigers were going to come last. He touched Priya's hand and she took off like an arrow from a bow.

'It's hopeless,' said Abby glumly. 'She's nearly half the length of the track behind.'

But Abby had underestimated Priya. Watching her, Connor could see that her skating action was more fluent than that of any of the other skaters, and she was catching them faster than he would have thought possible. And now he could see the three skaters in front of her slowing for the turn at the end.

'They're clumsy.' Toby was on the edge of his seat. 'They've all lost a lot of speed.'

'But they're moving again now,' Andy said. 'She'll never catch them.'

'Want to bet?' said Abby, leaping to her feet and yelling Priya's name. 'Look at her go! She hasn't slowed down for the turn at all!'

Priya was leaning into it, extracting every fraction of power from the edges of her skates. As she came out of the turn, Connor saw that she'd gained twenty metres and was closing fast on the third-placed skater.

'*Allez, la France!*' yelled Jay, and the others took up the cry as Priya overhauled one skater, and then a second.

'She's going to do it!' screamed Abby. 'Go on, Priya! Oh! How unlucky is that?'

Priya had simply run out of ice. Another two metres and she would have skated into the gold medal position. The skater from Switzerland collapsed to the ground, gasping for breath, but reached up to shake Priya's hand. The Tigers ran over to meet her.

'I'm sorry,' she said. 'It was just too much.'

'You're crazy!' said Connor. 'It was awesome, Priya! Silver is fantastic. We thought we'd come last.'

'Really?' Priya's face broke into an enormous grin, and Abby hugged her.

'We've made a great start,' Connor said. 'Now it's time for lunch, and then we'll see if we can all get our Snowsports Badges.'

'There's something else you have to do first,' said Julie, breaking in on the conversation. 'Rick and I need to see you all in the office for a moment. It's important.'

The Tigers took off their skates and followed Julie into the entrance hall, which was crowded with people. The office door was open, and inside they saw Rick talking to a woman with short blond hair and big gold earrings. Suddenly a small child came running out of the room and flung herself at Abby.

'Hayley!' cried Abby, picking her up and spinning round with her. 'Look at you! Fantastic!'

Rick beckoned them into the room and Julie closed the door. 'This is Mrs Barrett,' Julie said. 'She's Hayley's mum and she asked to see you all.'

'I just wanted to thank you for what you did for our Hayley. And for Lee too,' Mrs Barrett said. 'I won't forget it. Not ever.' Her eyes filled with tears and she blew her nose loudly. 'Go on, Hayley,' she went on. 'You know what to do.'

Hayley disappeared behind the desk and emerged with a huge bunch of flowers. 'These are for you,' she said to Abby.

Connor saw that Abby was blinking back tears.

'You know what, Hayley?' Abby said. 'You'll probably make a good Scout one day.'

'I wanted to go to Beavers,' she replied. 'But Lee said it was stupid.'

'Hayley!' interrupted her mum. 'I know what Lee did,' she said, turning to the Scouts. 'He won't be causing any more trouble for a while. I think he might actually have learned his lesson at last. And you're old enough to join the Cubs now, Hayley, just as soon as you like.'

'Well,' said Rick when Mrs Barrett and Hayley had left, 'now you're recruiting for the Cubs too! We've had a great response to the Search and Rescue talk. I think I can safely say you'll be getting your Community Challenge Badges.'

'But badges don't seem that important, do they?' said Abby. 'Not when you think what might have happened to Hayley and Lee.'

Julie smiled. 'Not the actual badges,' she said. 'It's the things you have to do to get them that are important, and the things you learn. You should be proud of what you've achieved. With a little bit of work you can all get your Snowsports Badges today – so go on and do it!'

'And how about one of you winning a gold medal for the Sixth Matfield?' added Rick. 'Sorry – I mean France, don't I? You nearly did it in the skating, and those points made quite a difference. The USA are in the lead at the moment, but we're not far behind in third place. I think we can win.'

CHAPTER 17

On the gentle slopes behind the Conference Centre, two young instructors from the ski centre were giving taster lessons to a group of enthusiastic Scouts. As the Tigers made their way to the taped-off skiing area, carrying their cross-country skis, Connor saw his dad and grandpa looking on with interest.

One of the instructors came over to them. 'My name's Jamie,' he told them. 'Would you like to join in?'

'We're hoping you can test us on our snow-sports knowledge,' Connor said. 'So that we can get our badges.'

Jamie was examining Connor's skis. 'Those are almost antiques,' he said. 'Do you mind if I have a look?'

'Those skis have travelled hundreds of miles across Norway, young man,' said Connor's grandpa, joining them. 'I hope you're not being rude about them!'

'No, sir,' replied Jamie. 'They're terrific. And you know how to use them?' he asked Connor.

'My grandpa taught us,' Connor said. 'We've used them here on an exercise . . .'

'Ah! You must be Tiger Patrol. I've heard all about you. How about you demonstrate the use of those skis for us, and then maybe you could let some of the others have a go?'

'We need to go out for half an hour,' Toby said. 'Then we'll all have logged sixteen hours on cross-country skis.'

'Well, that's half of your badge requirement. Then you'll need to answer some questions to check your knowledge. You understand what you're expected to know?'

They all nodded. Toby had been testing them relentlessly.

'OK, then,' Jamie finished. 'Let's see you skiing.'

'I'm coming too,' said Connor's grandpa. 'I didn't travel all this way just to watch other people having fun!'

'Oh.' Abby's face fell. 'You'll want your skis back.'

'No.' He shook his head. 'Those skis are yours now. And Chris wants you to keep yours too, Andy. You've earned them. And besides, it was a great chance for us to buy some nice new ones. Let's show them how it's done. We can just fit in half an hour before the sledging competition starts.'

The Tigers put on their skis and headed off into the country park, with Connor leading the way. They showed his grandpa where they'd found their casualties and they all took a turn at breaking trail. When they paused at the top of a rise, the Scouts were all breathing hard, but Connor's grandpa looked as if he'd just been for a gentle stroll.

'You're not bad,' he told them. 'If you keep it up for another forty years, you might be as good as me!'

They made their way back to the centre, laughing and chatting. As they neared the skiing area, they saw a tall figure come flying down a steep slope out in the park. He hit a small bump, took off and landed smoothly, never losing his shape. He stopped by the tapes, raised his goggles and stood chatting to Jamie as the Tigers approached.

'You're back,' said Jamie. 'This is Tom Glazer. I've been coaching him since he was three.'

'You!' said Abby. 'You never said you were a skier.'

'You never asked.' Tom grinned. 'Are you going to race in the downhill?'

'She's really good,' said Andy. 'I bet she's going to win.'

'Well, good luck,' replied Tom, taking off his skis. 'I'm off to watch the sledging.'

'Why did you have to say that to him,' Abby

asked Andy as Tom walked away. 'You could see how good he is.'

'He's not just good,' Jamie told them. 'He's one of the best. He's skied for Great Britain.'

'I thought it was the USA,' said Toby, confused, looking at the Stars and Stripes on Tom Glazer's leg as he vanished into the crowd.

'No.' Jamie shook his head, laughing. 'I mean, he really has skied for his country.'

'You see?' Abby groaned. 'He must think we're really stupid.'

'You never know,' said Connor. 'Anything could happen. He might fall over. In the real Winter Olympics people fall over all the time.'

'He probably won't,' replied Abby. She smiled suddenly. 'But you're right. There's always a chance. Let's get these forms filled in.'

The Tigers completed their questionnaires and then hurried off to the sledging competition. Abby and Andy weren't taking part in this, so they stood with their families and watched the others hurtling down the run.

'Where's Dad?' Abby asked her mum. 'Why isn't he here?'

'He's been held up,' she replied. 'The motorway was closed, but he's on his way. He should be here any time now.'

Abby crossed her fingers inside her pockets as Andy shot footage of the sledgers. Maybe she wouldn't actually win the skiing, but she did want her dad to see her try.

One by one the Tigers came down the run, all using Connor's sledge. Jay had been working on it, making adjustments to the steering and applying new wax to the runners with the help of Connor's grandpa, who'd arrived from Manchester in the middle of the week. With three sledgers still to go, Jay took hold of it and pulled it to the top of the hill.

'We did our best,' Connor said, joining Abby and Andy, 'but none of us is in the top three. 'Come on, Jay!' he yelled, deafening Abby as Jay appeared at the top of the slope and they saw the starting flag fall.

Jay raced forward and flung himself down on the sledge. Instantly Connor could see that he was taking a different line down the hill to any of the other competitors. 'He's way out on the far side,' he gasped. 'What's he doing?'

'He's losing it,' said Andy, his eye glued to his camera's viewfinder.

Jay was much closer now, and Abby saw him grimace as he struggled to hold the sledge in line. Just for a second it was on one runner, and she was sure it would tip over, but somehow Jay held it together before flashing past them and crossing the line – to loud cheers from all the Sixth Matfield Scouts and their supporters.

They waited anxiously for the time to be written on the whiteboard, and then cheered again when they saw that it was a whole second faster than anyone else. There was more cheering a nervous few minutes later, when neither of the two final sledgers could beat Jay's time. The Tigers crowded around him, exchanging high-fives and congratulating him.

'Our first gold medal!' said Connor. 'Well done, Jay. I don't know how you kept it from going over.'

'Me neither,' Jay replied. 'But look – we're still not in the lead.' The helpers were writing up the points totals on the board. 'It's really close,' he said. 'The First Matfield have seventy-three points and we have seventy-one. The skiing's going to decide it.'

'It's down to Abby and Andy,' Connor said.

'But . . . Tom Glazer is in the First Matfield.' Abby was looking at the points and trying to work out what they needed to do.

'You get four points for a win,' muttered Toby, who was working it out on a notepad. 'Three for second, two for third and one for completing the course. Say Abby wins and Andy comes third. That would do it. Tom Glazer's the only one skiing for their team.'

'But if Tom wins, there's nothing we can do,' said Abby.

'They're drawing lots for the order,' Connor told her. 'You'd better go. Good luck!'

There were ten skiers in the competition. Abby couldn't believe it when she put her hand into the bag and pulled out the number ten.

'You're last,' said Andy. 'That's great! You'll know exactly what you need to do.'

Abby shook her head. She already knew what she'd have to do. She'd have to ski better and faster than she'd ever skied before. She'd have to beat someone who had skied for Great Britain.

She looked over at the crowd of spectators, but there was still no sign of her dad. She watched as Andy pulled out the number seven, and then it was Tom Glazer's turn. He smiled at her as he turned round. 'Nine,' he said. 'I go right before you, Abby.'

The Scouts from the First Matfield Troop gathered around him. Abby could tell from the way they were talking that they thought they'd as good as won the Olympics already. 'You know what?' she said to Andy. 'I think we're going to have to show them. Are you ready?'

'Almost,' Andy replied. 'I want to video as much as possible before it's my turn. I'm going to stop here.' They had climbed halfway up the hill.

'You'd just better be ready,' Abby told him. 'If you—'

'It'll stop me feeling nervous,' Andy said, and as soon as he mentioned being nervous, Abby felt the fluttering in her own stomach.

She climbed up to the top, where Julie was on duty as the starter, and watched the first three skiers make their runs. They were all slow and clumsy. There really was no danger from anyone other than Tom Glazer, who was standing a few metres away, looking relaxed and confident.

'Abby! Come down here!' Andy was climbing towards her, beckoning urgently. 'You have to look.' Abby slithered down the hill a little way.

'Here,' he said. 'Look through the viewfinder. Down there, beside your mum.'

Abby held the camera to her eye. It was wobbly and jerked around, but then she got the hang of it. There was Rick, intent on his stopwatch. There were Andy's mum and dad – and there was her own mum. And there, beside Mum . . .

She blinked and looked again, then found that her eyes were full of tears. It was her dad. He'd made it finally – just in time.

'I knew you'd be pleased,' said Andy. 'You *are* pleased, aren't you?'

Abby wiped her eyes. 'Of course I am,' she said. 'But you should be up there. You're skiing next.'

'Look after the camera,' said Andy. 'You can give it to Julie before you ski.'

With that, he raced off up the hill. Abby followed behind him. Andy clipped his boots into his skis, pulled on his helmet and adjusted his goggles. Julie lowered the flag and Andy was away, skiing brilliantly all the way. There were just a couple of moments where Abby knew he had lost time, but he was easily the best skier so far.

When he reached the bottom, he skied over to his mum and dad, and Abby saw him speaking to her dad, and pointing back up the hill. Abby waved, and her dad waved back; then she walked happily to the top. Another skier was on her way down, but Abby barely gave her a glance.

When she reached Julie, she was talking on her phone. She rang off and turned to Abby and Tom Glazer. 'It's all down to you two,' she told them. 'France is just in the lead at the moment, thanks to Andy. Are you ready, Tom?'

'Your friend was good,' Tom said to Abby. 'Very good, in fact. Are you as good as he is?'

'I'm better.' Abby gave him a big confident smile. 'Much better.'

Abby saw the way Tom looked at her. He might have skied for Great Britain, but she was sure she had just planted a tiny seed of doubt in his mind. He pulled down his goggles and settled into a crouch.

'Ready . . . Go!'

Julie dropped her flag, and Tom was away. Abby drew in her breath. Tom looked every inch a professional skier. His curves were smooth and tight. His body was streamlined.

'He's an expert, isn't he?' Julie said with a wry smile. 'It'll be no disgrace if you don't beat him.'

'Look!' Abby exclaimed. 'He missed that turn. He lost it, just for a split second.'

'Really? It looked pretty good to me. Hold on, I'll just get the time.' There was a brief pause as she spoke into her phone. 'He's in the lead. He was half a second faster than Andy.'

Suddenly Abby had hope in her heart. On a slope like this she knew she was more than a second faster than Andy. And Tom had made a mistake. She could do it, but everything had to be perfect.

'Ready . . .' said Julie. 'Go!'

Abby took off. She had picked her route as she

watched the others. Slightly to the left to avoid lifting off . . . a tight curve to the right, the wind rushing past her ears as she moved on, turn after turn, faster and faster, her edges biting solidly into the snow. There was no way Tom could have been faster than this. She made one last turn, and then there was a straight run, down towards the cheering crowd.

And then her ski hit something. Maybe a stone, maybe a twig.

Something hard.

Something that shouldn't have been there.

There was no time to react, no time to correct.

Suddenly she was tumbling over, and her left ski was cartwheeling into the air. She rolled, and felt her other ski hit the snow. The edge bit, and somehow she pushed herself upright. She was still travelling fast. She felt as if she was falling again, but at the very last moment she managed to lean in the right direction. There was the finish. If she could just stay upright for another ten metres . . .

She crossed the line and felt herself falling, rolling over and over in the snow.

She lay on her back as the other Tigers raced towards her. She couldn't have done any more. It had been going so well, and then . . .

'That was just amazing!' said Andy, helping her to her feet.

There was a long moment of silence, and then the timekeeper looked up from his stopwatch. 'You've done it!' he said to Abby. 'Even with that fall you were half a second faster.' He turned to the spectators. 'France are the champions!'

The Tigers crowded round Abby and exchanged high-fives, followed by everyone else in the Troop.

Abby's dad ran over and lifted her into the air. 'Awesome skiing,' he said, hugging her tightly. 'I don't know how you stayed upright.'

'Dad!' Abby cried, ridiculously pleased. 'Put me down! I have to get my medal. We all do.'

Jack Holmes, the District Commissioner, was presenting the medals. The spectators gathered round and the ceremony began. Abby was the last to receive her medal.

'That was a magnificent performance, young lady,' Mr Holmes said as he placed the medal around her neck. Jay stood beside her with his gold medal. Priya had the team silver for skating, and Andy a bronze. 'I gather that your entire patrol has acquitted itself very well in this snowy emergency we've been having.'

He turned to the crowd. 'You saw this young man's movie this morning,' he said. 'They did all the right things. It seems to me they've been very well trained, first of all by their Scout Leaders' – he held a hand out to Rick and Julie, who got a warm round of applause – 'and secondly by our friends from the Matfield Lowland Search and Rescue team, who have also helped to organize today's events.'

There was an even bigger round of applause for Rob, Evie, Pete and the others.

'Don't forget,' called Abby, 'they need lots of volunteers!'

There was laughter and more cheering. 'We haven't had snow like this for fifty years,' Mr Holmes finished. 'So I expect the Sixth Matfield will be Matfield Winter Olympic Champions for a long time to come!'

'Olympic Champion, eh?' said Abby's dad afterwards, giving her another enormous hug. 'That sounds good to me.'

'It might even happen for real one day,' said Tom Glazer, coming up and shaking Abby's hand. 'You were amazing, Abby. Congratulations.'

'Thanks.' Abby felt a rush of happiness at being complimented by a national champion.

'What I don't understand,' said Abby's dad, 'is how you lot keep getting into these adventures? Last time you were lost on the moors. Now you're rescuing people from frozen lakes. Whatever next?'

'I've been thinking about that,' put in Connor. 'I reckon we should have a word with Rick. I'd like to try paragliding – or go on a proper expedition.' He glanced at his grandpa. 'Maybe on the water.'

'How about street-sports or cycling?' suggested Jay with a grin.

'Or horse-riding?' Priya's eyes were shining.

'Or caving?' Andy pointed his camcorder at Abby. 'How about you, Abby Taylor?' he asked, pretending to be a TV interviewer. 'What would you like to do?'

'I don't really care what it is,' replied Abby happily, looking round at the smiling faces of the other Tigers. 'But whatever it is, I can't wait for it to begin.'

THE TIGER PATROL'S DIARY

FAVOURITE CONSTELLATIONS Notes from Toby

ORION

The Hunter. You can see his belt and his sword.

Brightest stars Betelgeuse and Rigel. Top left and bottom right.

The Orion Nebula is in the middle of the sword. Looks like greenish

mist through binoculars.

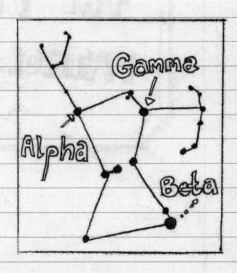

p.s. Betelgeuse and Rigel are also known as Alpha Orionis and Beta
Orionis.

CASSIOPEIA, THE PLOUGH AND THE NORTH STAR.

You can use the Plough or Cassiopeia to find the North Star.
I've drawn a picture (remember that the stars will be in different
parts of the sky at different times-all except the North Star -
that's always in the north!).

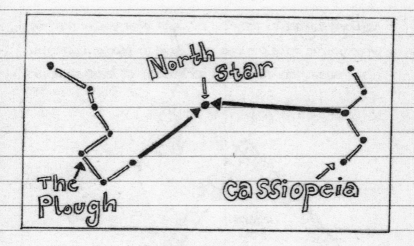

COMMUNITY CHALLENGE INFO Notes from Abby

First you have to decide what part of the local community you want to find out about and collect lots of information. Then you have to organize a visit. Sometimes it can just be your patrol, or it might be the whole Troop, but everyone has to help.

NB Don't forget to tell Rick or Julie what you're planning. When you've done the visit you have to report back. You also have to do community service for at least six hours.

TIPS FOR CROSS-COUNTRY SKIING
Notes from Connor

IMPORTANT THINGS TO REMEMBER ABOUT CROSS-COUNTRY SKIING.

DIAGONAL STEP.
You have to sort of hop from one ski to the other and dig in the pole on the opposite side. It's the main way of going forward.

HERRINGBONE STEP.
It's like walking like a duck with your skis turned out in a v shape. Gets you uphill. On the steeper hills you can go sideways and use you skis like steps.

GETTING UP AFTER YOU'VE FALLEN OVER.
Get your skis parallel and face uphill if you're on a slope. Hold your poles low down near the baskets and use them to push yourself upright.

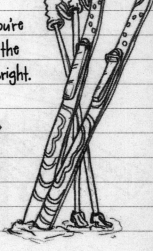

CONTENTS OF FIRST AID KIT Tips from the Tigers

Everyone on the expedition should have their own first-aid kit. Don't forget to keep it topped up if you use something. We've drawn a picture to show what should be in it.

DEALING WITH HYPOTHERMIA
Notes from Priya

1. Make sure you've prepared properly. Always have the right clothes and equipment. If you think someone's getting cold, the sooner you do something about it the better.
2. Find some shelter.
3. Remove wet clothes and replace them with dry spare things. Put on a hat and gloves if possible.
4. Insulate them from the cold - lay them out on a sleeping bag or mat and wrap them in a space-blanket or a survival bag. If it's serious then send for help. Don't leave the person alone. Warm them up with warm drinks and high-energy food. Look out for each other. If one of you has got cold it might happen to the others too.

BUILDING A SHELTER IN THE SNOW Andy's Tips

You can build a wall using big snowballs. The wall needs to be wide at the bottom. The wider the bottom wall, the taller you can build it, but even a low wall will shelter you from the wind. You can use plastic sheeting to make a roof if you have any. Weight it down with snow. You can use skis poles like tent poles. Use guy ropes to hold them upright.

NB WIND CHILL Getting out of the wind is really important. The

temperature might be just above freezing but in a 40kph wind it will feel like -6 degrees C. It's even worse if you have wet clothes.

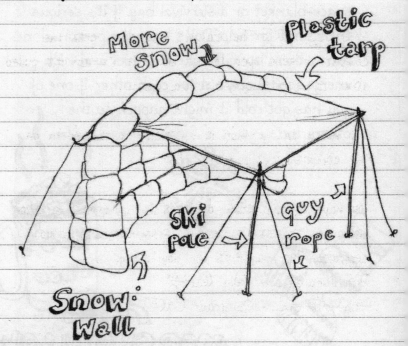

THREE KINDS OF NORTH Notes from Jay

There are three
Norths in navigation!

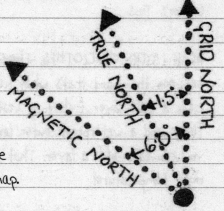

TRUE NORTH This is
where the North Pole is
and it's almost the same
as Grid North on the map.

GRID NORTH This is the north the grid lines on the
map point to.

MAGNETIC NORTH The Earth's magnetism pulls the
compass needle over to one side. In Britain it's pulled
about 3 or 4 degrees to the west.

NB north on the map is different to the north on
the compass!

You have to add some degrees for magnetic variation
when you transfer a bearing from the map to your
compass. The map tells you how many.
Grid Unto Mag - Add (GUMA)
Mag Unto Grid - Subtract (MUGS)

Keep Warm

KEEPING WARM IN THE COLD WEATHER

Connor's Tips

WEAR LAYERS OF CLOTHES. They'll trap layers of air between them and that's what keeps you warm. You might wear a base layer t-shirt or vest. Then a shirt and a fleece and a waterproof outer layer. If you get too hot you can take off a layer. That way you're always the right temperature!

WEAR A HAT AND GLOVES. You lose lots of heat through your head and hands.

KEEP YOUR CLOTHES DRY. That means put on a waterproof as soon as it starts to rain, and take off layers before you start to sweat. Wet clothes cool you down fast.

CARRY A HOT DRINK IN A FLASK.

HOT CHOCOLATE

Recipe for Hot chocolate (Serves 4-5 people)

INGREDIENTS

- 85g plain excellent (or as good as you can get) chocolate, broken into pieces
- 1 tablespoon of caster sugar, this is more to taste, so adjust for your own palette
- 1 teaspoon of vanilla essence
- 300ml of milk
- Marshmallows
- Some more freshly grated chocolate or cocoa powder, to sprinkle on top
- 2 warmed mugs

Put the chocolate pieces, sugar, vanilla essence and milk into a small, heavy-bottomed saucepan. Heat gently, stirring the mixture until the chocolate is all melted in. Carefully bring to the boil, whisking constantly with a whisk, until smooth and frothy.

Pour into the warmed mugs, top with marshmallows.

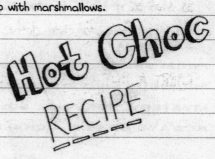

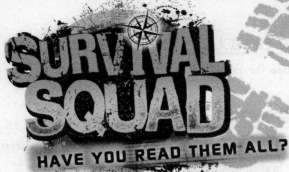

SURVIVAL SQUAD

HAVE YOU READ THEM ALL?

COMING SOON!

SURVIVAL SQUAD: NIGHT-RIDERS

SURVIVAL SQUAD: WHITEWATER

FROM SNOW RESCUES TO
MIDNIGHT BIKE RIDES AND
MYSTERY, SURVIVAL SQUAD ARE
ALWAYS UP FOR A CHALLENGE.